Contents

Turbulence

"I guess this is the place," I said a little nervously. This place gave me the creeps—it was so dark and isolated.

"The door should be locked," Mr. Eldridge said. "The security guard gave me a pass key for all the rooms." He held it out to me, but I already knew I didn't need it.

"It isn't locked," I said. I could feel warmer air coming from within the room. The door was ever-so-slightly ajar, open no more than a centimeter or two. I put my fingertips on the wood and pushed lightly. The door opened with a loud squeak of the hinges. I looked inside—and gasped.

The place was trashed! Drawers hung open, papers were strewn everywhere, and ancient-looking books lay scattered on the floor. "There's been a break-in!" I cried.

NANCY DREW
girl detective™

#1 Without a Trace
#2 A Race Against Time
#3 False Notes
#4 High Risk
#5 Lights, Camera . . .
#6 Action!
#7 The Stolen Relic
#8 The Scarlet Macaw Scandal
#9 Secret of the Spa

Available from Aladdin Paperbacks

NANCY DREW

girl detective™

#4

High Risk

CAROLYN KEENE

Aladdin Paperbacks
New York London Toronto Sydney

First Aladdin Paperbacks edition March 2004

ALADDIN PAPERBACKS
An imprint of Simon & Schuster Children's Publishing Division
1230 Avenue of the Americas, New York, NY 10020

Manufactured in the United States of America

20

Library of Congress Control Number 2003109057
ISBN-13: 978-0-689-86569-5
ISBN-10: 0-689-86569-4

High Risk

1

An Interesting Acquaintance

"More green beans, Nancy?" Mrs. Nickerson asked me.

My boyfriend, Ned, spoke up before I could answer. "Are you kidding?" he asked his mom. "Do you really think Nancy Drew would turn down a second helping of green beans?"

Ned was right. He knows that I think his mother makes the best garlic green beans in the entire city of River Heights. "I would love some more, please," I told her, holding out my plate.

"You're the town sleuth, aren't you, Nancy?" asked the Nickersons' other dinner guest, Colonel Lang.

"I do some detective work now and again," I replied. "But I don't have a license or anything."

"Nancy's being modest," Ned's father put in. "She's a bona fide supersleuth."

"In that case, I imagine she's sniffed out all the best dishes in town," Colonel Lang said. He held out his plate to Mrs. Nickerson. "May I have some of those green beans too?"

I grinned. Colonel Lang was funnier than I'd expected him to be. When Ned first told me about his dad's old friend who would be coming for dinner, he made it sound as if Colonel Lang would be a very strict, no-nonsense military man. But so far the retired colonel had been chatting and joking just like anyone else. I figured Ned must be remembering how he felt about Colonel Lang when Ned was a little boy. I could see how the tall, broad-shouldered man would be impressive in his air force uniform.

"Will you be in town long, Colonel?" I asked.

"I'll be flying in and out over the next few weeks," he answered.

"What for?" Yeah, I can be a little . . . forward.

He paused. "I'm here on . . . business."

Something about his tone made my detective senses tingle. He had hesitated slightly before mentioning his *business*. Was it something he didn't want to talk about?

"Won't that get expensive?" Mr. Nickerson asked.

Colonel Lang shook his head. "It would if I was flying commercial. But I've got my own plane now."

Everyone gasped with pleasure. "Your own plane!" Mrs. Nickerson exclaimed. "How exciting."

"Well, I was in the air force," the colonel joked. "I do know how to fly!"

"I wish you could teach me," Ned put in. "It sounds like a blast."

"I'd be happy to," Colonel Lang answered promptly.

I saw a flicker of surprise in Ned's eyes. "Oh, I was only kidding," he said hastily. "I know you probably don't have time."

"Nonsense," the big man said. "I would love to teach you. It will help repay the many favors I owe your father."

"Oh, really?" I asked, smiling at Ned's dad. He had been a highly regarded journalist in Washington, D.C., before moving to River Heights to take over the local newspaper. "Mr. Nickerson never talks about his Washington days. What kinds of favors did he do for you? I'd love to hear some stories."

"Yeah," Ned agreed. "Were you two involved in any political scandals together?"

Mr. Nickerson and Colonel Lang exchanged a charged look. I gulped in surprise. Ned and I had just been teasing them, but it seemed we'd hit a nerve.

"I don't know if you'd call it a *scandal*," Colonel Lang said guardedly. "Let's just say James helped me out of a jam once."

"And I shouldn't have," Mr. Nickerson said with a grin. "I compromised my journalistic principles for you."

Now *that* surprised me. Ned's father was completely committed to truth in journalism. In fact the main reason he'd wanted to be publisher of the *River Heights Bugle* was to ensure that true journalistic integrity wasn't lost on the local level. I couldn't help wondering what had taken place between these two all those years ago in Washington. I knew Mr. Nickerson would never be involved in something shady. But who knew about Colonel Lang? Maybe his easy grin hid a lot of secrets. They obviously weren't going to offer me the details though.

Colonel Lang raised his glass of water in a salute. "And I appreciated it. Now in return I'll teach Ned to fly." He pulled a personal digital assistant out of his jacket pocket and turned it on. "Let me write myself a note to clear my schedule," he said. "I'll call you with a time for our first lesson, Ned. What's the number here again?"

"Five-five-five, four-three-four-oh," Ned replied. The colonel entered it into his PDA.

"Would you mind if I tagged along during the lesson?" I asked. "I've never flown in a private plane before."

"Then you absolutely must come," the colonel

answered. "It's a completely different feeling than flying in a large jet."

"That would be great. Thanks," Ned said politely. He didn't sound as excited as I expected. He must just be tired, I thought. Of course he'd be psyched about learning to fly.

"So how are things in D.C.?" Mrs. Nickerson asked the colonel.

"Oh, the same as ever," he replied. "I'm sure you two don't miss the rat race."

"No, we're happy here in River Heights," Ned's mom admitted.

"What about you, James?" Colonel Lang asked. "You're not bored to death in a sleepy little town like this?"

"Certainly not," Mr. Nickerson replied. "We have our share of crime and intrigue here—just ask Nancy."

I nodded. "I sometimes think we have more than our share," I commented. "River Heights is a small city, but there's always a case for me to work on."

"I may have a new case for you soon," Ned's father said. "Chief McGinnis isn't interested, but maybe you will be."

I felt my cheeks flush and a tingle of excitement rush up my spine. The tiniest mention of a case to solve always causes that reaction. I can't help myself—I love a mystery! My two best friends, George Fayne and Bess Marvin, say I was born that way. I love to get to the bottom of things the same way Bess loves to put together a great outfit, and George loves a new electronic gadget. There are some loves you just can't fight.

"What's the mystery?" I asked breathlessly.

Mr. Nickerson chuckled. "Well, I don't know how much of an actual mystery it is," he replied. "But it's definitely getting on my nerves. I keep getting mysterious calls from a person I don't know. Three times in the past month, I've answered the phone to hear a voice telling me I have a package delivery that night."

"Is this your home phone or the phone at the *Bugle*?" I asked.

"My home phone," he replied. "And the person always hangs up without giving me any more information."

"Do you recognize the voice?" I asked. "Is it a man or a woman?"

Colonel Lang raised his eyebrows. "You really are a detective, aren't you?" he said, impressed.

I felt a little embarrassed. "I'm just curious," I said.

"Well, I'll take any help I can get," Mr. Nickerson put in. "To answer your question, Nancy, I don't recognize the voice. I think it's a man, but I can't be sure. It's a very gravelly voice, and the person only ever says three words on each call."

"What three words?" I asked.

"The person says, 'Package delivery tonight,' and then hangs up," Mr. Nickerson said. "At first I assumed it was a wrong number. But it keeps happening."

"Maybe one of these days a package will actually show up!" Colonel Lang joked.

"That's what our police chief said when I reported it," Mr. Nickerson replied. "He thinks it's just someone at FedEx who has laryngitis."

"That explains it," the colonel said. "With a voice like that, the guy has just been too sick to deliver the package!"

Everyone laughed, and I dropped the subject. There really didn't seem to be much of a mystery there.

"So what kind of stories are you working on at the paper?" Colonel Lang asked Ned's father.

"We have a big court case coming up," Mr. Nickerson answered. "The suit was just announced today. I'm sure your father will be getting involved, Nancy," he added. My dad is one of the most prominent lawyers in town, so he usually is involved in the big cases.

"What is it?" I asked.

"Rackham Industries is suing Evaline Waters for her land," Mr. Nickerson said. "They want to knock down her house and put up a new factory there."

I gasped. Ms. Waters was the librarian at River

Heights Public Library before she retired. She was the one who gave me my very first library card, and she was the one who showed me how to look up detective guides on the Internet. She was also very attached to her home—her family had lived there for generations. Ms. Waters's family was one of the oldest in the city. She was descended from the Native American tribe that originally settled the area.

"But what right does some big corporation have to Ms. Waters's land?" I asked.

"None of the details have been released yet," Mr. Nickerson said. "But I imagine there's some dispute about her ownership of the property."

"That's a shame," Ned's mother commented. "She's such a nice woman. I see her out working in her garden almost every day."

"It's true," I said. "She'd be devastated if she had to move."

"Well, let's hope Rackham loses their suit," Mr. Nickerson said. "Although they have a mighty good lawyer on their side."

I groaned. "Don't tell me," I said. "Deirdre's father."

Mr. Nickerson nodded. Remember how I said my father was a very prominent attorney? Well, there's another very prominent attorney in town—Mr. Shannon, the father of my old nemesis, Deirdre. She and I have been rivals ever since elementary school. I don't really have anything against her, but she's never liked me. She takes every opportunity to snub me, especially when I'm with Ned. She has a big crush on him, and she can't forgive me for being his girlfriend. Plus, our fathers are frequently on opposite sides of big lawsuits. I wondered if the Evaline Waters case would be one of those times.

Ned glanced at his watch. "We should get going, Nancy," he announced. "Our movie starts in twenty minutes."

"Okay." I pushed back my chair. "Thanks for dinner, Mrs. Nickerson. It was delicious."

"Aren't you sweet," she said.

"No, I'm full," I joked. "No popcorn for me at the theater!"

Colonel Lang stood up to shake my hand. "It was a pleasure to meet you, Nancy," he told me. "It's not often I see a hard-boiled detective as young as you!"

I smiled. "Thanks for letting me sit in on your flying lesson with Ned," I told him. "I can't wait!"

He nodded. "See you then."

Ned and I made our way to the door and headed outside just as the sun was setting over the river. I stopped on the front porch to look at it for a moment. The entire sky was filled with thick bands of vibrant red. Ned put his arm around my shoulders. "It's beautiful," he said, looking at the sunset.

"It sure is," I agreed. "Usually sunsets make me feel peaceful. But it's hard to be at peace when there's such an injustice in the works."

"You mean Evaline Waters?" Ned asked. He knows me well enough to see when I'm preoccupied by something.

"Yeah," I said. "We just have to help her keep her home. If my father's not on the case, I'm going to make him get on it!"

Ned laughed. "And when Nancy Drew puts her mind to something, you can be sure she'll get her way."

2

Intriguing Errands

"Hop in!" I called to Bess and George. They were sitting on the porch swing in front of Bess's house when I pulled into the driveway. As they trooped down the steps, I couldn't help marveling at how different my two best friends were. Even though they're cousins, George and Bess are total opposites. For one thing, they look completely different. Bess has shoulder-length, golden blond hair and sparkling blue eyes, and she's always perfectly made up and dressed to kill. George keeps her dark hair short, wears no makeup to accent her big brown eyes, and dresses strictly for comfort. I think the reason we make such a great team is that I fall right in between them.

"I have to sit in the front," Bess announced as she

opened the car door. "My skirt would get wrinkled by scrunching into the backseat."

George rolled her eyes and climbed into the back. "That's why people wear jeans to run errands," she told her cousin.

I grinned at them. "Thanks for coming along with me," I said. "Hannah gave me a long list of things to get done in the next few days, and it will go a lot faster if I have company." Our housekeeper, Hannah Gruen, has lived with me and Dad since my mother died when I was three. She's a member of the family—and she expects me to help out with the running of the house. So this week I was taking care of most of her usual errands while her family was in town.

"Where to first?" I asked, backing out of the driveway. "The cheese shop or the dry cleaners?"

"Cheese shop!" Bess and George chorused. I knew they would say that, because Harold Safer, who owns the cheese shop, always gives away free samples. As I headed downtown, I filled my friends in on my dinner at Ned's house the night before.

"Flying lessons!" George cried when I got to that part. "Ned is so lucky!"

"I know," I said. "Though he didn't seem as into it as I was. I'm so happy Colonel Lang is letting me go along." I was driving past the library as I said this, which reminded me of Evaline Waters.

"I found out something else last night," I added. "Rackham Industries is trying to kick Ms. Waters off her property."

"What?" cried Bess. "Her family has lived there forever."

"I know," I replied. "I feel awful for her. How about we pay her a visit after the cheese shop?"

"Sounds good to me," George said. "We should let her know we'll support her any way we can."

I pulled into the parking lot behind Safer's Cheese Shop and we all climbed out of the car. "Brace yourselves," I warned my friends as we headed for the door. "Mr. Safer just got back from New York two days ago."

Bess gave a good-natured groan. Mr. Safer may love cheese, but he loves Broadway shows even more. In fact his main passions in life are Broadway shows, sunsets, and cheese, in that order. I thought of the beautiful sky I'd seen the night before. Maybe I could distract him from telling us about the shows he'd seen in New York by bringing up the sunset I'd seen right here in River Heights.

As we opened the door, a bell rang out the first few notes of a melody from *The Sound of Music*. We were clearly the first customers of the day—the shop was empty. Mr. Safer stood behind the counter, slicing some Jarlsberg and placing it on crackers to put out for his customers. "Girls!" he cried when he saw us. "What a wonderful way to start the morning."

"Hi, Mr. Safer," we all said. I handed him Hannah's list of cheeses. "We have an extra-big order this week," I told him. "Hannah's family is having a reunion, and she's providing the food."

Mr. Safer's eyes widened as he scanned the list. "Well, that *is* going to be a lot of food," he said.

I nodded. Hannah's family is huge.

"So let me tell you all about New York!" Mr. Safer sang happily as he turned away to begin filling my order. "I saw four new shows."

"This cheese is delicious," George said, trying to change the subject. She took another bite of Jarlsberg.

"Of course it is," Mr. Safer said. "Now, the first day I got to Manhattan, I went straight to a matinee—"

"Look how red the rind of this cheese is," I interrupted, pointing to a wheel on display inside the glass-front counter. "It reminds me of the sunset last night."

Mr. Safer gasped. "Did you see it too?" he cried. The Broadway shows were forgotten. Bess wiggled her eyebrows at me and George gave me a tiny thumbs-up. One thing we all knew about Mr. Safer was that he could talk about musicals for hours. Sunset talk usually only took up a few minutes. "Wasn't it astonishing?" Mr. Safer asked.

"It really was," I said truthfully. "I've never seen it so red."

"You know what they say," Mr. Safer replied. "'Red sky at night, sailors' delight!'"

"What does that mean, anyway?" Bess asked. "What's so delightful about it?"

"Well, for one thing, it's delightful to look at," Mr. Safer said. "But it's part of an old saying—'Red sky at night, sailors' delight; red sky at morning, sailors take warning.'"

"It's from the days before weather reports," George put in. "When sailors on the open ocean needed to know if a storm was approaching, they'd look at the sky. A red sky basically means there aren't any clouds. It's a clear sky."

I was impressed. This must be one of the facts George stumbled across on the Internet. She is a total computer junkie, and one of the best hackers around. But she also just finds out odd little bits of information during her journeys online.

"Why does it matter if it's red at night or in the morning?" I asked.

Mr. Safer handed me my first bundle of cheese and continued with the rest of the order. "Because if the sky is red at night, you're looking west—at the sunset. That means there are no clouds on the horizon, and there won't be a storm."

"Most weather comes from the west," George added.

"Exactly!" Mr. Safer agreed, thrilled to have a helper in his audience. "But if you're looking at a red morning sky, you're looking east. That means there's clear weather ahead of you. But it also means a storm might be following the clear weather, since that's the typical weather pattern."

Bess wrinkled her nose. "That doesn't seem very scientific," she said.

I laughed. "It isn't," I told her. "I doubt it worked very well for the sailors."

Mr. Safer finished wrapping up Hannah's cheese and gave it to me. "I think weather satellites do a much better job," he confided. "But I'd still rather look at the sunset than at a weather map!"

"Me too," I said, paying him. "Well, we're off. Thanks, Mr. Safer!"

"But I didn't get to tell you about the musicals I saw!" he cried.

"We'll have to hear about them next time," Bess said sweetly, batting her eyelashes at him. No man can be offended when Bess is involved, and Mr. Safer was no exception. He smiled back at her.

"Okay then," he said. "You girls have a good day."

"You too," we all called as we headed out the door.

"Whew! Close one," George joked, leading the way to the car.

My mind was already on our next stop as I got behind the wheel. In no time at all, I was pulling into the driveway of Ms. Waters's lovely Victorian-style home. It was situated on a small hill right next door to the library. Usually Ms. Waters spent her mornings gardening, but today she was nowhere to be seen. My friends and I climbed the steps and rang her ancient doorbell.

Evaline Waters answered a minute later. Her salt-and-pepper hair was usually pulled into one neat braid that fell down her back. But today wisps stuck out all over the place. There was a smudge of dirt on her cheek, and part of a cobweb on her arm. "Why, hello, Nancy," Ms. Waters said, her face breaking into a smile when she saw me. "Bess, George. What a pleasant surprise."

"Hi, Ms. Waters," I replied. "Did we come at a bad time?"

"Of course not!" she cried. "Why would you think that?"

"Because you're a mess," George said bluntly. Bess elbowed her cousin in the side while I stifled a laugh. George believes in telling the truth—she'd rather be practical than polite.

Ms. Waters put a hand to her hair and smiled. "I

guess I am," she said ruefully. "I've been up in the attic all morning."

"How come?" I asked.

"Oh, I'm tearing the house apart," she said, "looking for the deed to this property."

"Because of Rackham Industries?" I asked. "We heard about the lawsuit. We wanted to come lend our support."

Ms. Waters motioned for us to come inside, and we followed her into the large, comfortable living room. Even though the house was Victorian style, it was furnished with the retired librarian's eclectic taste. Native American rugs hung on the walls, while the furniture was made of dark wood in a colonial style, and the carpet on the floor was a bright yellow shag. Somehow it all worked.

"You girls are so sweet," Ms. Waters said. "I know if I could only find the deed, I could prove that they have no right to my property."

"What exactly is Rackham's claim, if you don't mind my asking?" Bess said, her brow knit in concern.

"They say my property line is in a different place than I've always thought it was," Ms. Waters explained. "According to their maps, the house is built right on top of the property line. That means I only own the land under the living room and not the kitchen!"

"That doesn't seem right," I said. "Why would your ancestors have built the house right on top of the property line?"

"They didn't," Ms. Waters replied. "I know where the property ends. I just can't prove it."

"Do you want some help looking for the deed?" Bess asked.

Ms. Waters sighed. "I'm afraid it won't help, dear," she said. "I've searched everywhere. It's no surprise—my parents weren't very organized, and they owned the house before I did. They never figured out how to file important documents."

I found it hard to believe that superorganized Evaline Waters had come from a disorganized family. "Then how did you become such a great librarian?" I asked.

"It was my way of rebelling," she told me with a wink. "I wanted to be the opposite of my mother!"

"Do you really think the deed is lost for good?" George asked.

"I fear it is," Ms. Waters said.

"I can try to find a copy of it on the Internet," George offered. "A lot of cities put their public records online."

"I already checked," Ms. Waters said. She's surprisingly computer literate for someone her age—she had to be, working at the library. River Heights has one of the most state-of-the-art libraries in the whole county. "My property has been in the Waters family for so long that the original deed is gone, so they had nothing to scan in. It was lost in the flood of 1902, when the city hall floated away down the river."

"Wow," I said. "Your family owned this land even then?"

"Oh, longer than that," she said. "In fact, this is the third house that was built on the land—the first one fell apart on its own, and the second one was too old and small to be modernized with bathrooms and such and had to be torn down."

"But this house has to be almost seventy years old!" George cried.

"Seventy-three," Ms. Waters said. "That's why I can't believe anyone would want to take it from me. Why can't they build their factory somewhere else?"

"I don't know," I said. "But we'll do everything we can to help you. I'm going to ask my father about your case tonight."

"Oh, Nancy, that would be such a help," she said in a trembling voice. "I'm a strong character, but I have to admit that I don't want to fight this battle on my own."

"You won't have to," I assured her.

"Absolutely not. We'll help," Bess said. "Without

you, none of us would even know how to read!"

Ms. Waters chuckled. "I don't think that's true," she said, "but I appreciate your help."

"I'll let you know what my dad says," I told her as we headed out the front door. From the high porch I had a good view of Ms. Waters's land. Something in the far corner of the backyard caught my eye. "Ms. Waters, what's that?" I asked, pointing to a crumbling stone wall.

She squinted into the sunlight. "Oh, that's the old house," she said. "Not the last house. The very first one. It was really just a one-room cottage, the first place my ancestors built when they claimed the land."

"Which land is Rackham claiming that they own?" I asked.

"Everything from the kitchen on in this direction," she said, sweeping her arm across the backyard and the old house.

"That's it!" I cried. "That should help us clearly establish the property lines. If the original house was built all the way over there, then your family definitely owned the land past the middle of your house. Rackham has no claim to it."

"But they have a deed that says they do," she said.

"Their deed is wrong," I said confidently. "And we'll prove it."

• • • •

When I got home from running Hannah's errands, I found a note on the kitchen counter. In Hannah's neat handwriting, it said that I should call Ned. Grabbing an apple from the bowl next to it, I headed up to my room and dialed 555-4340. Ned answered on the second ring.

"Nickerson residence," he said in a strained voice.

"Ned?" I asked. "Is that you?"

"Oh, hey, Nance," he replied, his voice relaxing. "Sorry. I thought you might be our mystery caller again."

"You mean the package delivery guy?" I asked, remembering his father's story from the night before.

"Yup," Ned said. "Apparently he called again last night right after you and I left. My dad tried to get his name, but he just hung up."

"That is strange," I commented. "Was your father mad?"

"Kind of," Ned admitted. "I think at first he thought the whole thing was sort of funny. But now it's getting on his nerves."

"I don't blame him," I said. I thought telemarketers were annoying enough. But if this guy wouldn't even let Mr. Nickerson get a word in, how was he ever going to find out he had the wrong number?

"There's good news," Ned said. "Colonel Lang has

time for a flying lesson this afternoon. I was hoping you'd get back in time."

"We're going flying?" I cried. "What time?"

"Right now, if you're ready," Ned replied. "I'll pick you up on my way to the airport."

"See you soon, then," I told him. I hung up the phone and did a little dance around my room. Soon I'd be flying high!

3

The First Lesson

"Where are you?" I murmured, pulling back the living-room curtain to peer outside for the fifth time. I had run straight downstairs to wait for Ned. I just couldn't wait to get up in that plane! But he was obviously taking his time.

Just as I let the curtain drop, I heard a car pull into the driveway. Grabbing my bag, I ran for the door, yanked it open—and ran straight into my father.

"Whoa, slow down!" he cried, his handsome face breaking into a smile. "You almost bulldozed me!"

"Sorry, Dad," I said. "You're home early."

"Actually I just came back to get a change of clothes," he said, indicating a coffee stain on his tie. "I'm due in court in half an hour."

I grinned. When it comes to klutziness, Dad and I are two of a kind. It's a good thing he has at least a hundred ties!

"Where are you off to in such a hurry?" Dad asked.

"I'm going flying," I said excitedly. "Mr. Nickerson's friend is a pilot and he's giving Ned a lesson. They said I could tag along."

"Sounds like fun," Dad said. "Having a good day otherwise?"

"Yup. Except I'm worried about Ms. Waters," I told him.

He nodded. "I had a feeling I'd be hearing about that from you," he said. "I called Evaline not ten minutes ago and offered my services."

I threw my arms around him. "You're the best, Dad!" I cried.

"I'm not sure how much help I'll be," he cautioned me. "Evaline doesn't have much of a leg to stand on. Clearly that land has traditionally been considered hers, but she has no proof of ownership."

"We found remnants of the original Waters house at the edge of the property," I told him. "I thought maybe that could help establish property lines."

"Or it could just mean that the Waters ancestors built the house on land that they didn't officially own," he said. "It's difficult when you're dealing with such old claims. Most of the documentation is lost."

I frowned, chewing on my lip. I'd been so sure that that crumbling old house would help! "It's not fair," I said. "That original house had to be at least a hundred and fifty years old. It's like an archaeological ruin." Even as the words left my mouth, I had a new idea. But right at that moment, Ned pulled into the driveway.

"Gotta fly!" I joked, giving my dad a quick kiss on the cheek. "See you later."

"Have fun—and be careful!" Dad replied, waving at Ned before he disappeared into the house. As I started down the driveway, I pulled my cell phone from my bag and hit the speed dial number that George had programmed in for me. If she hadn't made my cell as easy to deal with as possible, I knew I'd never have the patience to use it.

I climbed in beside Ned and mouthed a hello while the phone rang. He rolled his eyes good-naturedly. Ned is used to my strange ways—he knows that when I have a hunch, I have to act on it immediately. He put the car in reverse and backed out, starting the drive to the airport.

"Hi, Nancy," George said after a moment. Gotta love caller ID. "What's up?"

"I have an idea," I told her. "Can you get on the Web and research historical-landmark laws for River Heights?"

"Sure," she said. "Why?"

"Well, that original Waters house should count as historically interesting, don't you think?" I said. "It must be the oldest foundation in the whole city!"

"Good thinking," George said. "I'll call you back later."

I thanked her and hung up. Then I bounced in my seat all the way to the airport, anticipating the plane ride. Ned laughed at me, but he didn't seem nearly as excited as I was. "Aren't you looking forward to this?" I asked. "Just think, maybe you'll get your pilot's license and then we can go up flying anytime we want."

"It takes a lot of lessons before you get your license," Ned told me. "I'm not sure I'll ever do that."

"But it'll still be fun, even with a flight instructor," I said. "And Colonel Lang is cool."

"You think so?" Ned asked. "I figured you'd find him suspicious."

"Why?" I asked.

"Because he doesn't like to talk about his past," Ned said. "And you're intrigued by even the hint of a secret."

I laughed. He was right. Colonel Lang did seem to be a man with secrets, but I still liked him.

Ned pulled into the River Heights Municipal Airport. The airport can handle smaller jets, but most people use it for their private planes or to take flying lessons. We climbed out of the car and walked into the small commercial-flight hangar. There were a few small planes in the giant barnlike building, one with its side panels open as a man examined its engine. We headed over to the row of dusty counters that lined the wall near the door. Two different flight schools operated out of this airport, and each one had its own counter with a sign on the wall. One sign said HARBERT'S FLIGHT TRAINING with the word *flight* in neon. The other had a tasteful hand-painted sign that read LEARN TO FLY WITH BELTRANO. Colonel Lang stood near this counter, chatting with a petite red-haired woman with an athletic frame. As we drew closer, I could see that she was older than I had thought—probably in her fifties.

"Nancy Drew, Ned Nickerson, this is Janice Mallory," Colonel Lang said as we approached.

Janice stuck out her hand, and I took it. She had a firm handshake and a big, friendly grin. "I've heard of you, of course," she told me. "You're our very own homegrown detective! Not here on a case, are you?"

I blushed. "Nope. I'm just here to have fun," I told her.

"That's what I like to hear," she said.

"Janice is the manager here," Colonel Lang told us. "She oversees the commercial side of the airport—the flight schools and the scheduling of private planes."

"Without her, we'd all be flying into each other in the sky!" joked a voice from behind me. I turned to see the tall, good-looking man who had been tinkering with the plane engine. He looked about forty and he wore a cocky grin.

"Without me, you'd spend all your time doing stunts and forgetting to teach classes," Janice joked back. "Folks, this is Frank Beltrano, one of our flight instructors," she told us. Then she made introductions all around. When Frank shook hands with Colonel Lang, I was surprised to see that he was at least five inches taller than the air force man. In spite of the height difference, though, there was something similar in their bearing—they both stood up straight with their shoulders back, and they both radiated confidence.

"Were you in the air force, like Colonel Lang?" I asked Frank.

He shook his head. "No, I learned to fly in the navy."

Colonel Lang glowered at him. "A navy man, hmm?" he asked in a fake threatening voice. "We may have some trouble up there." Everyone laughed, and the colonel clapped Frank on the shoulder.

"You kids are learning to fly?" Frank asked us.

"Just me for now," Ned replied.

"I'm only here for the ride," I said. "Though I'd love to learn sometime."

"Well, if you ever decide to take lessons, you give me a call," Frank said with a wink. He leaned over the counter and fished a business card out of the pile of papers on the other side. "Here's my number," he added, handing me the card.

"Thanks," I said. As I put the card in the pocket of my jeans, a short, balding man came bustling into the hangar. He hurried over to the counter and stood waiting impatiently for us to finish. He was clearly upset about something—sweat beaded his upper lip, and he tapped his foot unconsciously as he stood there.

Janice glanced over at him. "Excuse me," she said to us. "You kids have a great time!"

"Thanks," we both said. Colonel Lang led us away from the counter, but I glanced over my shoulder to watch Janice approach the man. He began yelling about something before she even opened her mouth.

What could he possibly be so upset about? Frank Beltrano stepped up to Janice's side to help her deal with the outraged man. The guy had turned practically purple in his anger.

"Nance—," Ned said just as I tripped over a gigantic cord on the floor. I started to fall, but Ned caught me easily. "Watch out for the wire," he finished with a smile.

"Thanks," I answered. "I guess I was distracted. I wonder what that man wanted."

"That's the drawback of being a sleuth," he said. "You're always on the lookout for suspicious behavior."

"Right now I'm not looking at anything but *that,*" I retorted. Directly in front of us, Colonel Lang had stopped before a sleek, shiny plane. It had been painted a deep green color, and it had two yellow stripes all the way around, and two more down the wings.

"It's a beautiful plane," I told the colonel. "A Piper Meridian, right?"

"That's right," Colonel Lang said. "You have a good eye. Hop in!"

Soon enough I was strapped into one of the two backseats while Ned buckled himself into the pilot's seat. He looked a little pale as Colonel Lang taxied slowly out of the hangar. From the copilot's seat next to Ned, he could control the plane as well. Once we got out into the sunlight, the colonel stopped the plane and began going over the instrument panel, explaining the purpose of each switch, knob, and gauge. I listened carefully, drinking in the information. Ned took notes in a small notepad.

"You won't be able to look at that while you're flying," the colonel said. "So make sure you memorize all this."

"Yes, sir," Ned said seriously.

"Now, this may sound basic," Colonel Lang said, "but the most important piece of equipment in the cockpit is this." He gestured to a small microphone in the middle of the control panel.

"What is it?" Ned asked.

"It's the radio," the colonel said. "This is your lifeline, because it's your connection to people on the ground and to other pilots in the air. Whenever you get into trouble, you radio for help. The controllers on the ground will be able to guide you."

Ned nodded, writing it down.

"I'd like you to handle the radio on our first flight," Colonel Lang said. "You have to get used to talking while you fly. The important thing to remember is that you don't do anything in a plane without letting the controllers know about it."

"Otherwise everyone would be flying into one another, right?" I asked.

"Potentially," the colonel agreed. "At a small airport like this one, there's not much danger. There are so few planes that you can see them all just by looking up into the sky. But it's still procedure to run everything by the tower."

I glanced out the window at the tower. It was really just a two-story building near the end of one of the two runways.

"The radio will connect you to the tower, and also to the main flight-school hangar," Colonel Lang said. "Okay, Ned, ask for permission to take off."

Ned carefully flipped the switch to turn the radio on. "Piper Meridian to tower," he said into the microphone. "Requesting permission to take off." He released the Talk button and glanced at the colonel, who shot him an approving nod.

"Copy, Meridian," a voice crackled over the line. "You're clear on runway two."

The colonel taxied to the end of the runway, then built up speed as he headed down it. Before I knew it, we were in the air. Colonel Lang talked the whole time, explaining to Ned everything he did. But once we were airborne, it was hard for me to hear from the backseat. I turned my attention to the scenery below.

This was different from flying in a big commercial jet because we were flying much closer to the ground. From here I could pick out details on the land and recognize buildings we flew over. I spotted George's house first, a block away from our elementary school. The school looked so tiny from up here! I could see a group of children playing on the swings in the playground. Next I caught sight of Bess's house—and Bess herself out on the driveway. She had the hood of her mother's car open and was tinkering with the engine.

Soon I spotted Evaline Waters's home. I checked out her property. From above, it looked neatly marked. All around the edges of her lawn grew a low, tangled hedge. I could make out the faint perimeter of the stone foundation and the crumbling wall of the original house. It was clearly inside the hedge.

"Okay, I think that's enough for our first lesson," Colonel Lang said, pulling the wheel to turn the plane back toward the airport. I felt a rush of disappointment, but Ned smiled.

"Yup, any more time and I might get information overload," he joked.

Once on the ground, the colonel taxied the Meridian back into the hangar. Janice was chatting with a client near the Harbert's Flight Training counter, and Frank Beltrano's plane was gone. I couldn't help taking a look around for the angry man who'd been here before, but there was no sign of him.

As Ned did a postflight check on the plane with Colonel Lang, I turned my cell phone on. There was a message from George. "Nancy, you're a genius," she said happily. "It took some creative Internet searching, but I found it—a zoning law that will protect Ms. Waters's property as a historical landmark!"

4

Legal Hope?

"I have to stop for gas," I told Bess and George the next morning. Once again I was running some errands for Hannah with my friends.

"Gas? What's that?" Bess joked.

"Are you sure you'll remember how to pump it, Nancy?" George teased me.

I stuck my tongue out at them as I drove toward the gas station. Because my car is a gas/electric hybrid, I get really good mileage. I don't have to fill it up with gas nearly as often as my friends have to fill their tanks.

"Tell me more about this zoning law," I said to George. "How specific is it?"

"I don't know," George admitted. "I didn't find the actual wording of the law. I only found a mention of the existence of the law. It was in an old article about the town charter. The writer didn't cite specifics; he just said there was a law still on the books from back in the early nineteenth century that would protect the original town buildings even if all that was left of them was a single stone of the foundation. I guess there had been a big fire recently, and the original town inhabitants wanted to be sure they wouldn't lose their land if their buildings burned down."

"So all we have to do is find the actual law, double-check the wording, and tell Nancy's father about it," Bess said. "I bet he'll get this case dismissed in no time."

"It's not that simple," George replied. "This is an old law that hasn't been used in more than a hundred years. I doubt the mayor even knows about it. It's not on any of the River Heights government Web sites—I checked."

"What are you saying?" I asked, turning into the gas station on the corner of River Street.

"I'm saying it's going to be hard to track down the wording of the law," George replied. "I think we have to find the actual piece of parchment that it was first written on."

I thought about that. An old, important document would be kept in a special place . . . but where? The town hall? A museum? Suddenly I knew the answer. At least, I knew how to *get* the answer. "Luther Eldridge," I said.

George raised an eyebrow. "What about him?"

"He knows everything about River Heights history," I replied. "If anyone will know where to find that document, he will."

I thought about Luther as I climbed out of the car and opened the gas tank. He was the father of my best friend from first grade, Melissa. One day while Luther was busy volunteering at the local recycling center, Melissa, her mom, and her older brother were killed in a car accident. It had been devastating to all of us. Melissa's dad, Luther, was the only one left in his whole family. He'd never really recovered from his grief—he'd quit his job as a college professor and now he just stayed at home alone with his history books. In Melissa's memory, I visit him from time to time to make sure he's doing okay. Plus, over the years I've come to like him—he's a sweet man, and very smart. He would definitely be able to help.

I gazed out over River Street as I began to pump my gas. Almost immediately one car caught my eye. Well, really it was the driver who caught my eye—it was the angry man from the airport the day before! He was driving slowly along River Street, swerving a little over the double yellow line in the center of the road. And no wonder—he was barely even watching where he was going. His head was craned to the right as he stared at the sidewalk.

Who was this man? We would all be lucky if he didn't cause an accident. I finished pumping my gas, paid the attendant, and got back into the car. When I pulled out onto River Street, the angry man's green sedan was stopped at a red light three cars in front of mine. When the light changed, he suddenly veered across traffic and made a left turn. On a whim I followed him.

"Whoa!" cried George. "Slow down, speed demon!"

"Where are we going?" Bess asked from the backseat. "The post office is in the other direction."

"I'm tailing someone," I said, keeping my eye on the green sedan. The driver made another left, moving fast. I followed, staying far enough back to avoid catching his attention.

"Tailing who?" George asked, surprised. "Is there a case we don't know about?"

I blew a strand of strawberry blond hair out of my eye. "Not really," I admitted. "In fact, not at all. But I saw this guy yesterday at the airport and he was furious about something. And now he's driving like a maniac." I made another left and followed him back toward River Street. "I just want to see where he's going."

Bess squinted out the window. "It looks like he's going in a circle," she commented.

She was right—we were back to almost the exact spot we'd started in. The gas station was just ahead on the corner. The angry man made another left back onto River Street, this time moving slowly. I pulled up close behind him. He was still staring at the sidewalk.

"He's looking for someone," I murmured.

"Maybe he dropped his wife off in one of the shops and he's circling until she comes out," George suggested. Like I said, she always goes for the practical explanation first. I couldn't help but smile.

"You're probably right," I said. "I guess there's nothing that strange about being angry and driving around."

"Let's ask Charlie," Bess suggested. "He's in Mason's parking lot."

I glanced into the small lot in front of Mason's Drugstore. Sure enough, there was Charlie Adams with his tow truck. Charlie is often my savior, because as infrequently as my car needs gas, I still usually forget to stop and fill up. Charlie has had to come to my rescue with a can full of gas on numerous occasions. He doesn't even charge me anymore!

I pulled into the gas station. Charlie spends his days driving all over River Heights, talking to just about everyone. Sooner or later everyone needs their car fixed, and Charlie's boss runs the best garage in the city. That all means that Charlie knows a lot about what goes on around here. I wondered whether he knew the angry man.

I parked next to the tow truck and we all got out.

"Hey, Bess, George," Charlie said. Then his eyes met mine and he blushed. "Hi, Nancy," he added.

"Charlie, I need your opinion," I said, getting straight to the point. "Have you noticed a green sedan on River Street today?"

"Yes." Charlie's expression grew worried. He takes helping me with cases very seriously. "Why? Has there been a crime?"

Bess giggled. "Only if bad driving is a crime."

"Bess is right. There's no case. I just think the man driving that car is acting strangely," I said. "Look!" The green sedan was pulling onto River Street again from the same side street as before. "He's just driving in circles."

"That's the thing," Charlie said. "He's been doing that for almost an hour. I was watching him even before you showed up. At first I thought he was looking for parking, but now I have no idea what he's doing."

We all watched as Angry Man pulled around the block again.

"Nancy, we'd better get going if you want to finish all your errands *and* visit Luther Eldridge," George pointed out.

"Okay," I agreed. "I guess I'll just have to resign myself to not knowing why that man is acting so weird."

"I'll keep an eye on him for you," Charlie offered. "I'll call if he does anything really suspicious."

"Thanks, Charlie," I said, getting back into my car. "You're the best!" Charlie blushed again.

Charlie gave a good-natured wave as we pulled out, and I headed straight for Luther Eldridge's colonial-style house on Spur Woods Lane. Mr. Eldridge's lawn was full of dandelions, and the car in the driveway was showing rust spots. But inside, the house was spick-and-span, with everything in its place. He was surprised to see us—he doesn't have many visitors these days, since he likes to keep to himself.

"Can I get you girls a soda or anything?" he asked as we sat down in his living room. On the mantel was a family photo. Seeing Melissa's smiling face in the picture made me sad. "No thanks," I replied. "I was hoping you could help us out with something."

"Another mystery?" Mr. Eldridge asked, his brown eyes smiling.

"Believe it or not, no!" I replied. "We're trying to help Evaline Waters hang on to her property."

"Rackham Industries is suing her for it," Bess put in. "They claim they own the land right up to the middle of her house."

Mr. Eldridge slowly shook his head, frowning. "That doesn't seem right," he said. "The Waters family has owned that land for generations."

"Ms. Waters can't find a deed to the property, and there's no record in city hall," George said.

"Ms. Waters's parents didn't seem to keep things like that in order," I explained. "But George found a mention of an old zoning law about historical landmarks. The trouble is, we need to track down the original document containing the law."

"Well, you could try city hall," Mr. Eldridge said. "But their archives only go back to the nineteen twenties. How old a law is this?"

"We think it's from at least a hundred and fifty years ago," George replied. "I didn't even know there were laws that old."

"That wouldn't be in city hall," Mr. Eldridge commented.

"Could it be in a museum somewhere?" I asked.

"I doubt it," he said. "It doesn't hold much interest, except to old historians like me."

"I think Evaline Waters would be pretty interested in it," Bess said.

"There's an archive at the university," Mr. Eldridge said. "My best guess is that this sort of thing would be there, if it's anywhere. Since the university was one of the very first institutions in River Heights, a lot of the old historical documents are there."

"Do you think we can get into the archive right now?" I asked.

"I guess my old ID might get us in," Mr. Eldridge said uncertainly. "If the place is even still open at all. I can't imagine that anyone other than security has been there in years."

"I'm willing to try if you are," I said. "It could help Mrs. Waters a great deal." Mr. Eldridge needed a little coaxing to leave his house. Finally he nodded.

"Great!" I said. "Let's go!"

Oddly, the university archive was just as empty as Mr. Eldridge had said it would be. The place was a small, overgrown brick building out in back of the library. The door had a heavy chain over it with a big padlock holding it shut. We had to find a security guard to unlock it for us, after he took a good look at Mr. Eldridge's old university ID. It took the man five minutes just to locate the correct key on his giant metal loop. He unlocked the door, conferred briefly with Mr. Eldridge, then left us.

"I don't think people come here much," Bess whispered as we stepped inside. The heavy wooden door slammed shut behind us with a dull thud. The only light came from a flickering fluorescent tube in the ceiling.

"No one is interested in musty old history anymore," Mr. Eldridge said sadly. "Now they want everything available on a computer screen at the touch of a button."

George shot me a smile. She was definitely one of the people Mr. Eldridge was talking about.

"How do we find the right document?" I asked.

Mr. Eldridge led the way to a big cherrywood desk in the center of the small entryway. On the desk sat a leather-bound logbook. When he opened it, dust flew up into the air, making me sneeze.

"This book should tell us how the archive is organized," Mr. Eldridge said, running his finger down the rows of handwritten entries. "Here we go! Laws, River Heights, 1837 through 1860."

"That's it!" I said. This was going to be easier than I'd thought.

"Room five, section F," Mr. Eldridge said, leading us down a darkened hallway. Along the hall were several closed doors, each with a small lightbulb at the top. The dim light barely illuminated the metal numbers tacked to each doorjamb.

At room 5, I found the number hanging upside down. It gave an ominous creak when I turned it to the right. "I guess this is the place," I said a little nervously. This place gave me the creeps—it was so dark and isolated.

"The door should be locked," Mr. Eldridge said. "The security guard gave me a pass key for all the rooms." He held it out to me, but I already knew I didn't need it.

"It isn't locked," I said. I could feel warmer air coming from within the room. The door was ever-so-slightly ajar, open no more than a centimeter or two. I put my fingertips on the wood and pushed lightly. The door opened with a loud squeak of the hinges. I looked inside—and gasped.

The place was trashed! Drawers hung open, papers were strewn everywhere, and ancient-looking books lay scattered on the floor. "There's been a break-in!" I cried.

5

Who Stole the Law?

Before Bess had even returned with the campus police, we had discovered that the document we wanted was gone. Once George and I gathered up all the paper from the floor, Luther Eldridge was able to make sense of the mess quickly and easily. Almost all of the papers came from sections E and F. None of the files in the other sections had even been touched.

Mr. Eldridge brought the logbook in from the front desk and we went through the contents of sections E and F, checking off those documents and books that were still here. When we were finished, the truth was clear: The only document stolen was the one containing the zoning law that would help Evaline Waters. I smelled a rat.

I was thankful that the university police were the ones who took our report. I didn't want to have to explain to Chief McGinnis what I was doing here. The River Heights police chief already often thinks I stick my nose in where it doesn't belong.

After we dropped Mr. Eldridge off, my friends and I drove home in silence. I knew they were trying to make sense of this situation, the same way I was.

"It had to be Rackham Industries who broke into the archive," Bess said finally. "They're the ones who want Ms. Waters's land. They're the only ones who would care about that law."

"But they're a huge corporation," George argued. "They're not going to resort to breaking and entering in order to get a tiny piece of land. They can just build a factory somewhere else."

"But if not Rackham, then who?" I asked. My detective work had taught me that the most obvious answer is usually the correct one, and Bess had a point about Rackham Industries. They stood to gain the most from the theft of this document. But George made sense too—it didn't seem likely that a company would open itself up to this kind of obvious criminal activity.

I was startled out of my thoughts by the sight of the green sedan we'd followed earlier. "Look!" I cried to my friends. "It's Angry Man's car." The sedan was parked along River Street in front of a shop with a Grand Opening banner hung in the window.

"Looks like he was just circling in order to get a good parking spot!" George said.

But something was nagging at the back of my mind. I glanced up at the new shop again, and that's when it all fell into place.

"I knew he looked familiar!" I cried. "Angry Man is the owner of the new antique shop!"

"Berring Antiques?" Bess asked. "I haven't been in there yet."

"I have," I said. I noticed another spot along the curb, and I pulled the car over to parallel park. "Dad and I went in last week, the day it opened. It was pretty packed, but Mr. Berring was there behind the counter."

"If he's got a store full of beautiful antiques that's doing good business, what's he so angry about?" George asked.

I finished parking and turned off the car. "That's just what I want to find out," I said. We all got out, and I led the way into Berring Antiques. The store was chock-full of gorgeous old wooden furniture, pieces of antique china, and shelves full of finely woven linens. It was getting toward closing time, so we were the only customers there. Mr. Berring seemed surprised to see us come in.

"Oh!" he said. "I was just about to put the Closed sign up."

"What a shame," Bess replied with a friendly smile. "I've been dying to take a look at the store."

"Well . . . ," Mr. Berring said. "I guess I can wait for a few minutes while you look."

"Thanks so much!" Bess cried. She grabbed George's arm and pulled her into an aisle containing antique picture frames.

"It's nice to see you again," I told Mr. Berring.

He gave an uncertain smile. "Have we met?" he asked.

"Well, not really," I said. "But I saw you at the airport yesterday. I hope you got everything straightened out there."

Mr. Berring took a step backward and knocked into a coat rack. It started to topple, but I reached forward and grabbed it before it fell. "I'm afraid you have me confused with someone else," Mr. Berring said. "I wasn't at the airport yesterday."

I looked into his eyes as he spoke, and he glanced away.

"Guess I must have one of those familiar faces," he added nervously.

I smiled at him. "I guess so," I agreed. "My mistake." But I knew I hadn't made a mistake—that had definitely been Mr. Berring at the airport. Now the only question left was, Why would he lie about it?

I was still wondering about that fifteen minutes later as we stood in line at the bakery. Hannah wanted two loaves of their special banana bread. Unfortunately, so did everyone else in town. Joshua Andrews, the baker, only makes it one day a week, and the lines are always long on banana bread day.

"I know it was Mr. Berring at the airport," I said aloud.

George laughed. "Of course it was him," she replied. "We all know you never forget a face."

"Maybe he has an identical twin," Bess said, only half joking. Vintage Bess: Even though we didn't know if Mr. Berring was up to anything illegal, she was trying to defend him. She never likes to think ill of anybody.

"Lying about it only makes him seem more suspicious," I pointed out. "What is he trying to hide?"

"Sticking your nose into someone else's business again, Nancy?" asked a sarcastic voice.

I turned and glanced into the familiar green eyes of Deirdre Shannon. She had gotten in line behind us, along with a guy I didn't recognize. That was nothing new—Deirdre changes boyfriends as often as some people change their clothes. She never keeps anyone around for very long. In fact, her longest-running crush has been on *my* boyfriend, Ned. I decided not to point out to her that by eavesdropping on my conversation, Deirdre was sticking *her* nose in *my* business!

"We're just chatting," I told her.

She tossed her jet-black hair over her shoulder and rolled her eyes. "Whatever," she said. "I heard your dad is up against mine . . . again," she commented.

Deirdre always tries to make it sound as if our fathers are having a fight, when in fact they're both just doing their jobs. "Well, they're on opposing sides in the Rackham versus Waters case," I said. "Their clients are at odds, but I would hardly say our fathers are *against* each other."

"My father will win," Deirdre said confidently. "That old lady can barely even prove that she owns any of that land."

"That's for the judge to decide," I said diplomatically. I always try to be polite, but sometimes Deirdre really annoys me. How could she have so little sympathy for Evaline Waters?

"I can't wait," Deirdre added. "Rackham Industries

is a big client—when Daddy wins this case, he says we can move to a bigger house."

"That sounds great, DeeDee," George said sweetly. She knows how much Deirdre hates being called by her childhood nickname.

Deirdre frowned at her, but didn't say anything.

I couldn't help wondering though. I didn't personally know Deirdre's father, but if this case really represented that much money to him, he must care about it a lot. Enough to steal?

"Did you hear about the break-in at the university archives?" I asked Deirdre. "A document was stolen that could have had an impact on the Waters case."

Deirdre yawned. "You always have the most boring gossip," she commented. "Why would you care about some smelly old archive?" She turned to her boyfriend, who was practically asleep on his feet. "Let's go. I'll send the housekeeper to stand in line."

The guy shrugged, and Deirdre led the way out of the bakery without even saying good-bye.

"That girl has the worst manners," Bess said. "Why did you ask her about the break-in, Nancy?"

"Well, if her father stands to gain a lot of money from winning the case, he has a motive for stealing that document," I said. "It was the only piece of evidence that could help Mrs. Waters."

"That's true," George agreed. "So if he got rid of it, your father wouldn't have a case."

Bess frowned. "You don't really think Mr. Shannon would break the law, do you?" she asked.

I pictured Deirdre's father. He was a tall, imposing man with broad shoulders and bushy eyebrows. I'd really only seen him in court when I went to watch my dad try cases. He'd never come to any of our school functions. "I know my father thinks that Mr. Shannon bends the rules sometimes," I said slowly. "But he's never said Mr. Shannon is unethical."

"Still, there aren't any other suspects," George pointed out.

"I know," I said. "And there aren't any other documents containing that law, either. I'm afraid Ms. Waters may lose her case."

"I've been thinking about that," George said. "And maybe there is another document that will help."

"What?" Bess cried.

"The law we're looking for was a town law," George explained. "It only applied to River Heights. But it would probably have been registered with the county, as well. So there may be a county document that mentions the town law."

"Then we should go to the archive in Silver Creek," Bess suggested. Silver Creek was a few towns away, and it was the location of the county government.

"It's a long shot," I said. "But that may be our only hope!"

6

Another Break-In

The next morning Ned and I arrived at the airport ten minutes early for Ned's flying lesson with Colonel Lang. I was excited to get back up in the air, but Ned seemed nervous.

"I don't think the colonel's here yet," he said as we walked into the hangar. "I didn't see his rental car outside."

I hadn't seen the car either. It was hard to miss—a bright red vintage Mustang in perfect condition. But I was kind of happy to find that we'd beaten Colonel Lang here. It would give me a few minutes to talk to Frank Beltrano, who was sitting behind his counter drinking a cup of coffee.

"Let's go say hi," I told Ned.

"You go ahead," he replied. "I'm going to keep an eye out for the colonel."

I watched Ned head back out the hangar door. He began pacing up and down in front of the doorway. Ned is usually very calm and unflappable. I wasn't sure why he seemed so keyed up today. I turned and walked over to Frank Beltrano.

"Good morning, Mr. Beltrano," I said. "Remember me?"

"Of course," he replied cheerfully. "Nancy Drew! Did you come to sign up for flying lessons?"

"No, I'm just tagging along with Ned again," I replied. "I saw your friend in town yesterday."

He looked at me blankly.

"Mr. Berring?" I reminded him. "We went into his antique store."

"I'm afraid you've lost me," Mr. Beltrano said with a shrug. "I don't know any Mr. Berring."

"Isn't that the name of the man who was here the other day before our lesson?" I asked, feigning confusion.

Mr. Beltrano shook his head. "I don't remember any man," he said. "Sorry."

I put on a smile. "My mistake," I said. I didn't know what to think. No one seemed to remember what had happened here the other day. But one thing

I've learned during all my sleuthing is to trust my own memory. I knew Mr. Berring had been here, and I knew Frank Beltrano had gone over to help Janice when Mr. Berring yelled at her.

"Nancy!" Ned called. He stood with Colonel Lang near the doorway.

"Guess I'd better go," I said to Mr. Beltrano.

"Have fun," he said with a friendly grin.

I jogged over to Ned and the colonel and we headed out onto the tarmac where the colonel's Piper Meridian was parked.

"Glad you could join us again, Nancy," Colonel Lang said. "We're just about to do the preflight check."

"That takes place on the ground, right?" Ned asked.

The colonel chuckled. "Yes. Most of the important parts of flying take place on the ground. You have to be absolutely certain that your plane is in working order before you take off. The flight is only as safe as the machinery."

Ned nodded nervously. "Where do we start?" he asked.

"At the cockpit," Colonel Lang answered. "Start there, and make a circuit of the whole plane until you come back to the cockpit."

After checking each instrument in the cockpit, we walked around the outside of the plane. "First we examine the propeller," the colonel explained. "Make sure the propeller switch is off."

Ned peered at the switch and nodded. "It's off."

"Okay, now we look at the propeller to make sure the area is clear," Colonel Lang said. "Ned, I want you to check every inch. Even the tiniest debris stuck in the machinery, or the smallest substance stuck to one of the blades, can throw the plane off in the air."

Ned's eyes were wide as he examined the propeller. It took a long time.

"Next we check the tires and brakes," the colonel said. "Look for cuts or punctures in the tires, and check for leaks from the brakes."

I bent to examine the tires, and my eyes scanned the ground for any sign of leakage. I wished Bess was here with me—she loves machinery. She would be so into this.

"Now we're going to examine the plane itself," the colonel announced. "Look closely for cracks or buckling of the metal. Even a hairline crack could be dangerous. Look for any signs of strain on the material or for rivets starting to pull loose."

"You're making me worried," Ned said. I couldn't tell if he was joking or not. "Listening to you, it seems like there's so much that could go wrong."

The colonel patted his plane affectionately. "This is a good bird," he said. "I trust her with my life. But that's because I make sure to check everything before every flight. It's part of being a responsible pilot."

"The point is to make sure everything *doesn't* go wrong," I told Ned. "Try to focus on that rather than on all the things that could break."

He nodded, but he still seemed nervous.

Colonel Lang continued the slow circle of the plane, pointing out where to check for loose wires, bolts that had worn down, and leakages. We moved the hinges on the wing flaps up and down to make sure they moved smoothly. We checked the oil and the fuel. We stood away from the plane and studied the alignment of the tires and the landing gear.

By the time we got in, I felt as if I knew every inch of the plane. I was familiar with all the pieces of machinery and I knew what each one did. Colonel Lang was right—it made me feel safer just knowing that I had checked every inch of it myself. But Ned looked a little overwhelmed.

During the entire flight I leaned forward in my chair to hear everything the colonel said. Ned kept his eyes on his notebook, writing furiously. I couldn't help smiling. Ned and I had never taken a class together before. We certainly had different ways of learning! I wanted to drink it all in. Watching the colonel was enough to make me remember all the things he was teaching. But Ned seemed to feel that he had to have it on paper so that he could study it later.

After we landed and did the postflight check of the plane, Ned and I walked Colonel Lang to his rental car. "I won't be able to give you another lesson for a few days, Ned," he said as he unlocked the door of the Mustang. "I'll be back in D.C. until the end of the week."

My heart sank a little. That long until we could fly again? But Ned just nodded. "No problem," he said happily. "Whenever you get back will be fine."

Colonel Lang gave us a little wave, then got in his car and pulled out.

"Do you want to go for ice cream?" Ned asked as we headed toward my car.

"Actually, I was thinking of doing a little investigative work," I admitted. "How do you feel about driving to Silver Creek?"

"What are we looking for there?" he asked, getting into the passenger seat.

"Another old document," I said. I had already filled him in on what had happened at the university archive the day before, and my theories on why and who. "George thinks there may be a list of laws from the different towns in the county. The zoning law we need would be mentioned there."

"If it could possibly help Ms. Waters, I'm happy to do it," Ned told me.

I smiled at him. He's used to my single-minded behavior when I'm on a case. This wasn't really a *case*, but it still had my full attention.

It took about half an hour to get to Silver Creek. As we entered the town limits, I called George to get directions to the archive. She was on the Internet on her computer, and on the phone with me. In no time at all, she'd located the Silver Creek Legislative Archive in the basement of the main courthouse. She gave me directions until I pulled up right in front.

"Thanks, George," I said. "You're better than GPS!"

I hung up, and Ned and I climbed the marble steps up to the imposing building. We passed between two white columns and stepped inside the cool, dark lobby. I told the security guard where we wanted to go and she gave us a map of the building. Ned and I walked through the metal detectors and located the small basement staircase in one corner of the lobby. As we descended, the lights grew dimmer.

"I'm getting the impression that every archive in the world is poorly lit!" I joked. "The one in River Heights was the same way." In fact, this archive had a lot in common with that one. For one thing, it was deserted. There was a thick layer of dust on the book labeled SIGN IN that sat on a small podium next to the door. I blew off the dust and wrote my name and the date. Then I pushed open the metal door and peered inside. It was dark.

"The lights are kept low to minimize the damage that light causes to the books and documents. There's a switch on each bookcase," Ned said. He reached past me and twisted a timer knob that turned on an overhead light. "It's the same in the library stacks at school." Ned goes to the university, and he spends a lot of time in the library. He loves reading so much, I'm surprised he hasn't started sleeping there.

I peered at the labels on the ends of the nearest bookshelves. They were dingy white index cards with handwritten titles, so I had some trouble reading them. But eventually I made sense of the layout of the room. "The county logbooks are in row S," I said. "And the ones from before 1900 should be in the drawers underneath the shelves."

Ned strode off into the dark room, twisting the knobs to turn on lights as he went. I followed, keeping my fingers crossed that we'd find a log of laws that included the one we needed. I could picture the relieved smile on Ms. Waters's face already.

"Here we are," Ned announced. "Row S—" His voice broke off.

"What's wrong?" I asked, rushing to catch up with him. Ned had stopped right at the entrance to row S. I peered around him and gasped. The entire row was filled with paper. The books had been pulled off the shelves and dumped haphazardly on the linoleum-tile floor, and all the drawers stood open, their papers spilling out in every direction.

"I can't believe it," I cried. "This archive has been broken into, too!"

"I'm going to call for help," Ned said, turning back toward the door. While he was gone, I made my way carefully through the mess to the drawer I'd wanted. It was completely empty. I glanced around at all the other papers and books strewn about. It was very similar to the scene at the university's archive. And I had a feeling that this entire mess was here to distract attention from the fact that only one document was missing—the one I wanted.

Had Deirdre's father done this, too?

Ned came back with two security guards, who took one look at the mess and chased us outside. We waited in the dark stairwell until a slim young woman with short red hair appeared. She rushed down the stairs, her eyes wide. She looked around, frazzled. "Are you the ones who found it?" she asked me.

"We found the papers and books all over the floor," I replied. I offered her my hand. "I'm Nancy Drew."

The woman pushed her hair back with a thin hand and smiled. "Kaylin Marshall," she said, shaking my hand. "I'm the assistant archivist for Silver Creek County."

"Ned Nickerson," Ned said, shaking hands. "I'm sorry about the break-in."

"I feel like it's my fault," Kaylin confessed. "I'm supposed to check on all the county archives every day, but I missed this one yesterday. I had a doctor's appointment."

"If someone stole archived documents, it's the thief's fault, not yours," I said.

"I know, but my boss will be angry with me," Kaylin replied. "Mr. Williams is always complaining about the lack of proper security at the archives."

"Is he the head archivist?" I asked.

Kaylin nodded. "Felix Williams, County Archivist. Haven't you ever heard of him?"

I shook my head, but Ned's eyes lit up. "Wait a minute! Is he that crazy guy who's always picketing the town halls all by himself?"

"That's him," Kaylin replied.

"My father does a yearly piece on him in the *Bugle,*" Ned told me. "Five days a week he spends his lunch hours walking around in front of different town halls in the county, carrying a big cardboard sign. He's been doing it for twenty years."

Kaylin rolled her eyes, but I thought it sounded kind of amusing. "What does the sign say?" I asked.

"'If you lose your history, you lose your mind.' He thinks all legal and historical archives should be kept under lock and key and that the public should never be allowed in," Kaylin explained.

"That seems sort of harsh," I said. "The public should have access to public documents, shouldn't it?"

"Of course," Kaylin said. "But Mr. Williams doesn't have much respect for the public. He thinks people will damage the documents. You know, spill soda on them and tear them by accident, that sort of thing."

"That's why he's on his crusade," Ned said. "My father's yearly piece details what progress he's made toward getting the archives locked up."

"Has he made *any* progress?" I asked.

"Nope," Kaylin said. "It's a lost cause—it wouldn't be right to prevent people from seeing public documents. Not that many people want to, of course."

"Well, I hate to say it, but Mr. Williams might have a point," I told her. "I don't think the public should be kept out of public archives, but he is right about the lack of security. What happened here proves that this archive should be locked, and there should be a guard posted down here to keep track of who comes in and out."

"You're right," Kaylin said. "And I'll be hearing about it from Mr. Williams for the next month!"

I smiled. "Do you mind if we come back inside

with you? We were looking for a specific document and I'd like to know if it's still here."

"Of course," Kaylin said. "What was it? Hardly anyone wants to see these old legal papers."

"A very old law from River Heights," I explained. "The original document was stolen from the university archive recently and I was looking for a log entry of it here at the county headquarters."

Kaylin's eyebrows shot up. "Stolen recently?" she asked. "Do you mean there's a rash of archive thefts?"

"If there is, Nancy will get to the bottom of it," Ned put in. "She's the best detective in River Heights."

Kaylin looked me up and down. "You don't look like a detective," she said.

"I'm just an amateur," I told her. "But I do manage to solve most of the cases I take on. And right now I'm trying to help a friend hold on to the house she's lived in all her life."

One of the security guards came out of the archive room. "It's all clear," he said. "There's no sign of forced entry. It seems as if someone just came in and made a mess."

"We just signed the book and walked right in," I said. "Couldn't someone else do the same thing?"

"Yes," Kaylin replied. "It's an open, public archive, although not a very popular one. Anyone can browse through the documents. But no one is allowed to leave with them."

"Security would have stopped anyone trying to leave with an archived document," the guard said. "No one was stopped, so we assume nothing was taken."

"I'll do a quick check, Nancy," Kaylin said. "I know this archive so well—it will only take me a minute to figure out if anything is missing."

As she disappeared inside, I glanced at the book. The last name listed was dated six months before. "This book was covered in dust when we signed in," I said to the guards. "Whoever did this didn't sign in. Do you have security cameras down here?"

They exchanged an embarrassed look. "No," said the one we'd been talking to. "So few people come looking for this archive that we don't bother with cameras."

"That will change after this," the other guard assured us.

Kaylin came rushing back out. "You're right, Nancy!" she cried. "The county logbook that covers the first half of the nineteenth century is missing."

"It must've been taken by the same person who stole the original zoning law document from the River Heights archive," I said, turning to Ned.

"Mr. Shannon?" he whispered.

"I don't like to think so," I whispered back. "But he *is* our best suspect."

"There's also another old document missing," Kaylin added. "It's an original county law banning pickle eating in the town hall."

I stared at her, wondering if I'd heard correctly.

"Pickle eating?" Ned asked.

Kaylin nodded. "Apparently the crunching was disturbing to the councilmen at the time," she said. "It's still a law, in fact. No one ever took it off the books."

"So if we eat a pickle at lunch, we're breaking the law?" one of the guards asked.

"Yup! You could receive a citation and have to pay up to two dollars in fines," Kaylin replied. "Of course, it's not enforced anymore."

"Are there a lot of laws like that?" I asked.

"You'd be astonished how many," Kaylin said, her eyes shining. "I'd be happy to tell you about them sometime. It's part of my job to know all the old, obscure laws. My office is a public resource—anyone can come in to learn about the county's history at any time."

"Sounds like fun," Ned said.

"Maybe we'll come back after I solve this case," I said. "I assume you're going to report the document theft to the police."

Kaylin sighed. "I'll report it," she said. "But I doubt that they can do much. I can't even imagine who would want to steal these crumbling old bits of paper."

"I'll let you know if I find out," I said. Ned and I left the archivist to her cleanup and headed back to the lobby.

"Should we call Chief McGinnis and tell him to check out Mr. Shannon's alibi for yesterday?" Ned asked as we walked down the courthouse steps.

I shook my head. "It wasn't Mr. Shannon," I told him. "He's not the document thief."

"How do you know?" Ned asked.

"Because he has a motive to steal the original zoning law document, and to steal the logbook that mentions that law," I explained. "But he has no motive to steal the pickle-eating law. He's not our thief." I stood for a moment, staring back up at the courthouse. "But then who is?"

7

At the Controls

"How was Ned's flying lesson yesterday?" my father asked at breakfast the next morning. I grabbed a muffin off the plate on the dining room table and began to nibble at it.

"Well, *I* liked it," I said. "But I'm not sure Ned had much fun. He seems sort of uninterested in flying. You would never believe how slow he was at the controls."

"Maybe he's nervous," Dad suggested. "Some people find the idea of flying to be terrifying."

"But learning to be a pilot was Ned's idea," I told him. "He asked Colonel Lang to teach him."

Hannah bustled in with a fresh pot of coffee. Her hair was sticking up every which way, as if she'd forgotten to brush it.

"Hi, Hannah," I said. "Um . . . how are you?"

"Don't get me started," she replied. "My two brothers kept me out talking until three o'clock in the morning! I'm exhausted." She finished pouring the coffee and went back into the kitchen. That explained her messy hair, she was probably still half asleep.

"When is Ned's next lesson?" Dad asked as the swinging door shut behind Hannah.

"Not for several days," I told him sadly. "The colonel is out of town."

"That's too bad," Dad said. "I can tell you really enjoy it."

A new thought struck me. "There was a flight instructor at the airport who gave me his card," I said, reaching for my bag. I fished out Frank Beltrano's business card and handed it to my father. "He gives private lessons. How would you feel about me learning to fly myself?"

Dad squinted at Mr. Beltrano's card, then looked up at me. "You'd be careful?" he asked.

I nodded eagerly.

"And you wouldn't pull any stunts? No doing loops or flying upside down?" Dad pressed.

Now he was just teasing me. "I don't think they teach you how to fly upside down until the second lesson at least," I joked.

Dad smiled. "Okay," he said. "Why don't we try five lessons, and then you can decide if you still like it enough to continue."

"Oh, Dad, thank you!" I cried, getting up to give him a hug. "I can't wait!"

"Then I'd better call right now," he said, reaching for the cordless phone that sat on the table. He dialed the number printed on Frank Beltrano's card and waited. I sat back down, but it was hard to stay still. I couldn't believe I was going to take flying lessons!

When Mr. Beltrano picked up, Dad arranged for five lessons, jotting down the dates and times on the back of the business card. He hung up and handed the schedule to me. "Since you're so eager to get started, Frank said he can take you up this afternoon at five."

"Today?" I said. "That's terrific!"

All day long the only thing I could think of was my flying lesson. I spent a few hours in the morning helping Hannah decorate the local firehouse hall for her family reunion. And in the afternoon I checked in with Chief McGinnis about the break-in at the university archive. He had no leads, and he didn't seem to find the case terribly pressing. After all, nobody really cared about some old piece of paper.

"Ms. Waters cares about it," I told him. But the police chief said there was really nothing he could do. It was going to be up to me to find out who the archive thief was. Unfortunately I didn't have much to go on either.

When the late afternoon rolled around, I was raring to start my pilot lesson. I arrived at the airport fifteen minutes early to fill out all the paperwork required to take lessons from Frank Beltrano. But he wasn't there. I waited around by his counter until five o'clock, when my lesson was supposed to start. Then I made my way to the office at the back of the hangar, where Janice Mallory works.

"Hi, Ms. Mallory," I said. "I was wondering if you've heard from Frank Beltrano. He was supposed to give me a lesson at five."

"Oh, Nancy, I'm so sorry," she replied. "I didn't know you were here. Frank's running late, I'm afraid. He'll be delayed by about an hour."

I was surprised to hear that. "If we don't go up until six, it will be dark by the time we finish the lesson, won't it?" I asked. "Will we be able to fly in the dark?"

"The sun goes down pretty late this time of year," Ms. Mallory assured me. "And Frank knows what he's doing. You'll be finished before dark."

"Okay," I said. "Thanks." I returned to the counter, sat cross-legged on the dusty floor, and waited. After about half an hour, Frank Beltrano came rushing in.

"I'm so sorry," he called.

"That's all right, Mr. Beltrano," I said.

"Call me Frank," he told me. "Let's go!" He bustled off toward his plane, a Cessna Skyhawk. This plane was a bit smaller than the colonel's. It was white with a thick band of purple around the body. "I know you've watched a few of Colonel Lang's lessons," Frank said. "So you're a bit more advanced than the average first-timer." He quickly ran through all the instruments and gauges, explaining the use of each one. This was a different plane from the colonel's, so many of the instruments were in a slightly different place. Still, I remembered almost all of them from Colonel Lang's descriptions, and I was proud of how much I knew. Frank was impressed too.

"Now we're ready to take off," he said. "Strap yourself in." He helped me adjust the seat and the shoulder harness so that it fit snugly. I noticed that his own safety belt hung loosely around his tall frame.

"How come yours is so loose?" I asked.

Frank looked embarrassed. "This is a situation where you need to do as I say, not as I do," he joked. "I can't stand a tight seat belt. It makes me feel claustrophobic. But it's dangerous to wear your belt loose like I do. You should always make sure it's securely tightened around you."

I thought it was a little irresponsible for him to set such a bad example, but he'd been a pilot for years. I guess he felt comfortable with his loose seat belt.

Frank had me radio the tower for permission to take off. He went through the takeoff procedures, which were only slightly different from those in Colonel Lang's plane. I soaked it all in, watching cvcry move he made.

Once we were up in the air and flying straight, he gave me a grin. "You ready to take the controls?" he asked.

"Yes!" I said immediately.

"Today we're going to practice flying straight and level," he said. "And maybe you'll do one turn."

"Okay," I said.

"Straight and level sounds easy, right?" he asked.

I nodded.

"Well, it's not," Frank said. "In fact some pilots never get comfortable with it."

"Why?" I asked.

"Because it's hard to shake the habit of trying to fly by sight," he explained. "People want to look at the nose of the plane and try to keep it straight by the way it looks. Like driving a car."

"That makes sense, though, doesn't it?" I said.

"It makes sense in a car," he replied. "But there are different things to keep in mind up here. For one thing, the air pressure. Cars don't have wings, and they don't really need to deal with wind."

I smiled. "That's true."

"Also, you can't see where the wings are by looking at the nose of the plane," he explained. "The nose might be straight, even if one wing is lower than the other. It takes a lot of practice just to keep the plane level."

"Okay," I said. This was going to be harder than I thought.

"I've got us going straight and level right now," Frank said. "I want you to take your wheel and I'm going to switch control over to you. The trick is to make sure you're not putting more pressure on one side of the wheel than the other."

I nodded, holding the wheel. I'm right-handed, so my tendency is to use more strength with that hand. I consciously focused on keeping the pressure even with my left hand.

"Okay . . . ," Frank said, pressing a button. "You're in control."

I couldn't believe it. I was actually flying! All by myself, I was piloting a plane through the air. For a minute or two I concentrated on keeping the wheel straight so that the wings would remain even. Finally I began to relax and get used to the way it felt.

Flying was such an incredible rush that I almost missed the sunset. I glanced up from the controls, squinting against the bright red light. And then it hit me—the absolute beauty of the sky around me. We were flying low over the river, and the water below reflected the vibrant red streaks of light in the sky. I couldn't wait to tell Harold Safer about it. I felt as if I was actually a part of the sunset!

The moment was spoiled by a loud chirping sound. It was the cell phone in Frank's shirt pocket. I jumped a little, but my brain instantly adjusted, reminding me that I was at the controls of a plane. I couldn't let anything distract me or break my concentration. I opened my mouth to tell him that I felt confident at the controls, so that he'd be comfortable answering his phone. But Frank had already pressed the Talk button. Clearly he'd been expecting this call.

I couldn't help feeling a little surprised that he hadn't checked with me first—what if I lost control of the plane? But I knew he could take over flying from the copilot's seat, and of course he would hang up if anything bad happened. It must mean that he trusted my ability as a pilot.

And I was beginning to think I made a pretty good pilot too!

Back on the ground, I thanked Frank for the lesson and headed home. Driving the car felt strange after being in the air. I was in such a good mood that I practically danced up the driveway.

"Nancy!" Hannah called from the front door. "Phone for you!"

"Oh!" I forced myself to stop thinking about flying and hurried to take the cordless. "Hello?" I said.

"Nancy, it's me," Bess answered me in a whisper. "We've got news."

"What news?" I asked. "Why are you talking so quietly?"

"I'm hiding in the ladies' room," Bess whispered, as if that explained everything.

"Hiding from who?" I asked.

"Deirdre Shannon," she replied. "We've been following her."

"What?" I cried. "Why?"

"Well, you decided her father couldn't be behind the archive thefts. But Deirdre has just as much motive as he does. She wants him to win the case against Ms. Waters so that she can have a new house."

That much was true. "But Bess," I said, "why would Deirdre steal the document about eating pickles?"

"That's what I wondered," Bess said. "But George said that DeeDee always hated pickles—"

A door slammed in the background, and I heard George shushing Bess. I couldn't help smiling at the thought of the two of them hiding in a restroom with the cell phone.

"Is Deirdre in the ladies' room too?" I asked.

"Yeah." Bess's whisper was almost too quiet to be heard.

"What has she been doing all day?" I asked.

"She's—aaahhh!" Bess's quiet voice turned into a scream of horror. Then the phone went dead.

8

Bess and George's Stakeout

I took the corner of Western as fast as safety allowed. I could hardly wait to get to George's house. Ever since that phone call the day before, I'd been worried about my two best friends. Neither one of them had called me back, even though I'd left messages with their parents. I knew if anything was seriously wrong, their families would have called me. But I still needed to find out what had happened!

As I drove down River Street, I glanced up at Berring Antiques. The metal security gate had been pushed aside enough for someone to enter, and there was a dim light on in the back of the shop. Mr. Berring's green sedan was parked right out front. I figured he must be opening up for the day. I pulled to a stop at the corner to let a group of schoolchildren cross with their crossing guard. While I waited, a flash of red caught my eye on the other side of the street. I peered through the group of kids, trying to see what the red thing was.

Then the children made it across, and I found myself looking at a vintage red Mustang parked on the other side of River Street. It was Colonel Lang's rental car! I drove past slowly so that I could look into the car. The colonel wasn't there.

I frowned, trying to remember what the colonel had said about going out of town. I'd thought he was gone for a few days, but maybe he was back already. Or maybe he hadn't left yet.

I put him out of my mind as I turned onto George's street. To my surprise, Bess was already there. Both of them stood on the front porch while George locked the door. I guessed they were on their way out somewhere.

I pulled into the driveway and got out. "Where have you been?" I called as I walked over to the porch. "You guys didn't call me back last night!"

George and Bess exchanged guilty looks. "Sorry, Nancy," Bess said. "We got home kind of late—"

"What happened when we were on the phone?" I pressed. "Did Deirdre discover that you were following her?"

"You could say that," George replied. "We were hard to miss. Bess made quite a splash."

Bess's peaches-and-cream complexion turned a dark shade of red, and she shoved her cousin in the arm. "Don't make fun of me!" she scolded. But a smile pulled at the corners of her mouth.

"Will someone tell me what's going on?" I cried. "I've been worried sick about you two."

"We didn't mean to scare you," George said. "We followed Deirdre all afternoon yesterday. She went into about twenty stores—"

"There's a sale at Sloane's Shoes," Bess interrupted. "I saw the perfect pair of slingbacks to go with those black capris we bought you last month."

George cleared her throat.

"Sorry," Bess said.

"So anyway," George continued the story. "We went to a bunch of different stores, but she didn't go anywhere near an archive, or even a bookstore. It was all about clothes."

I couldn't help smiling. George doesn't have much patience for shopping. Tailing Deirdre must have been torture for her.

"Then Deirdre went into the ladies' room in the department store," Bess put in. "She had about five shopping bags with her, so we thought she might have hidden the legal documents in one of the bags."

"So you followed her into the restroom," I said.

"Yes," Bess replied. "And she dragged all her bags into the stall with her, so we couldn't look in them to check for the documents."

"As if she'd be walking around with old stolen legal papers in her shopping bags anyway," George said dryly. I laughed. I certainly appreciated how much work my friends had done in tracking their suspect, but I just couldn't imagine Deirdre stealing legal documents in the first place.

"We hid in two stalls across from her so she wouldn't see us," Bess said. "That's when I called you."

I nodded.

George took up the story. "When Deirdre went out, she left one bag behind. So my cousin here went into the stall to check out the bag."

"Well, what else was I supposed to do?" Bess asked. "This is while I was talking to you on my cell phone, Nancy."

George continued. "And then she leaned over to look in the bag—"

"Just as George decided to push open the stall door right into me—"

"And she fell over and dropped her cell phone into the toilet," George finished.

I burst out laughing. Now I understood Bess's horrified scream. I could picture her face as she watched her cell phone fall into the water. "Did Deirdre hear you?" I asked, still giggling.

"Are you kidding?" George said. "Everyone in the store heard us! They had to get a janitor to fish the phone out of the toilet since it was partway down the pipe. Then Bess had to explain to Deirdre how she managed to drop a phone into a toilet when she was pretending not to be in the restroom at all, and Deirdre accused her of trying to steal the bag of clothes she left behind. . . . It was a mess."

"Did you ever get to look in the bag?" I asked.

George nodded. "In all the confusion, I sneaked a peek inside. It was nothing—just a really ugly skirt and a few pairs of socks."

"I don't think Deirdre is our thief anyway," I said. "She's just not organized enough to come up with a plan to steal documents from two different archives. I doubt she'd even know what an archive was."

"You're probably right," Bess replied. "It was just a hunch. So what did you do yesterday?"

"I took my first flying lesson!" I announced.

Bess and George both gasped. "Alone?" George asked. "Or with Ned?"

"On my own," I said. "Colonel Lang is out of town for a few days . . . well, at least he said he would be. . . ." I trailed off, thinking of the colonel's rental car parked on River Street.

"Earth to Nancy Drew," Bess said. "You were telling us about flying."

"Right. Sorry," I said. "The colonel is away so he can't give lessons for a while. And Ned doesn't seem that into flying anyway. But I love it. So I asked Dad if I could take private lessons."

"And he said yes?" George asked. "Your father is so cool."

"I'm signed up for five lessons with a flight instructor I met at the airport," I told them. "It's so much fun."

"What kind of plane do you fly?" Bess asked.

"A Cessna Skyhawk," I replied.

"What does Ned think about all this?" George asked. "Is he going to tag along on your lessons like you did on his?"

That question startled me. In fact, my decision to take lessons on my own had happened so quickly that I hadn't even had time to tell Ned about it. Now that George had mentioned it, I felt bad. Why hadn't I checked to see if Ned wanted to come along with me on my lesson the day before?

"I didn't tell Ned," I admitted. "It just didn't even occur to me. He really doesn't seem to like flying that much."

George and Bess stared at me, surprised. "You didn't tell him?" Bess repeated. "Won't he be mad?"

"I don't think so," I said. "Why would he care if I'm taking flying lessons?"

George scrunched up her face. She does that when she's thinking hard. "I don't know," she admitted. "I guess it just seems like he might be jealous, since it was his idea first."

"Yeah," Bess put in. "How will Ned feel if you get your pilot's license before he does?"

I thought about that. Ned and I were always supportive of each other, but usually we didn't do the same things. This was the first time we would be in direct competition with each other. Would that change our relationship?

"I don't even know if I'll get my license," I said slowly. "That takes a really long time. And if I do, I doubt Ned would be jealous. That would be silly. We can both get our licenses if we want to."

Bess nodded. "You're right," she said. "If there's one thing that Ned isn't, it's silly. You two will be the most high-flying couple ever!"

I relaxed a little. Bess knew what she was talking about—I'd never seen Ned do a silly thing in his life. And he had never been jealous of my accomplishments. He would be fine with me taking lessons.

"We were on our way to get Bess a new cell

phone," George told me. "Do you want to come along?"

I shook my head. "I'm helping Hannah do the final setup for her family reunion tomorrow," I said. "I just came by to make sure you guys were okay."

"Do you want us to do anything on the Evaline Waters case?" Bess asked. "Since our adventure yesterday turned out to be useless . . ."

"I can't think of what to do next," I admitted. "We have missing historical documents, but only some of them are relevant to Ms. Waters's lawsuit. The archives have such lax security that the guards have no idea who was even in them! The thief could be anyone in River Heights or Silver Creek."

"Or anywhere in between," George said, discouraged.

I sighed. "I need more information," I said. "Maybe I'll go visit Chief McGinnis later and see if he's gotten reports of any other documents missing."

"Phone us if you need anything," Bess called as I walked back down the driveway to my car. I waved to them, got in, and backed out into the street. Driving back down River Street, I could see that Berring Antiques was now fully open for the day, and Mr. Berring's green sedan was still out front.

So was Colonel Lang's red Mustang. Something about that bothered me. Why would he tell us he was going out of town if it wasn't true? Had he let someone else drive his car while he was away?

When I got home, Hannah handed me a platter of vegetables. "These have to go in your car," she said. "My hatchback has no backseat." I grabbed the cordless phone and hit Ned's speed dial number. Then I carried the veggie plate out to my car and balanced it on the seat while I listened to his phone ringing.

I had to tell him about my private pilot lessons as soon as possible. I didn't think he'd feel angry or jealous, but I did think he might be insulted that I hadn't told him about them. Ned's mom answered the phone.

"Hi, Mrs. Nickerson," I said. "It's Nancy calling for Ned."

"Oh, hi, Nancy," she replied. "I hear you went flying with Ned and the colonel."

"I did," I told her. "It was amazing! I bet Ned can't wait to go again."

"I'm afraid he'll have to wait," she said. "Colonel Lang won't be back in town until next week."

I opened my mouth to tell her about seeing his car on River Street, but something stopped me. Clearly the colonel wanted us all to think he was away. Of course, someone else could have rented the car, but my sixth sense told me this was something suspicious. It wouldn't do any good to blow his cover with the Nickersons. But I couldn't help wondering why Colonel Lang would be lying to some of his oldest friends.

I was so distracted by this that I barely even noticed when Ned got on the line. He asked me if I wanted to catch a movie that night and I said yes, then we hung up. I decided I wouldn't tell Ned about my flying lessons until we met with Colonel Langley, and just have fun for the night.

9

Flying High

Over the next several days I helped Hannah survive her family reunion, and I helped Dad prepare for the preliminary hearing on the Evaline Waters lawsuit by pulling documents, making copies, and anything else he'd let me do. It didn't look good for poor Ms. Waters. She'd never managed to find the deed to her property, so Dad didn't have much to go on in arguing her case. I decided to pay her a visit to cheer her up. But first I stopped at the police station.

I hadn't even gotten inside when I ran into Chief McGinnis. He took one look at me and his already-flushed cheeks grew even redder. I think the chief likes me, but he never likes to see me at his station. That's because it usually means I've discovered something he didn't know about, or broken a case before he has.

"Hello, Ms. Drew," he said. "I'm on the way out."

"Is there something wrong?" I asked.

He ran a plump hand through his thinning hair. "Just some graffiti on the fence near the middle school," he mumbled.

"Let me guess," I said. "It says 'Go, Wildcats' and it advertises the annual picnic and softball game."

"That's right," the chief said, disgusted. "You kids have had that silly tradition since before I even moved to River Heights. Why can't you just hang a banner instead of using paint?"

"I always thought the school should stop reporting it and just leave the mural up," I told him. "That way no one would have to repaint it the next year."

The chief just looked at me balefully. "Was there something you wanted, Nancy?"

"Yes, actually," I answered cheerfully. "I was wondering if you've had any breaks in the case of the archive thief."

"I'm not on that case anymore," he said. "After you stumbled on that theft over in Silver Creek, the county police took over the investigation here in River Heights, as well." Was it my imagination, or did he look a little relieved?

"Do you know who the county police chief is?" I asked. "I guess I should give him a call."

"You can give *her* a call," he said. "Her name is Donna Wagner. But I don't think you'll find out anything new. None of the stolen documents have any real value, so it's difficult to find a motive. All Chief Wagner can do is tighten security at the archives, especially after the theft yesterday."

My mouth dropped open. "Yesterday?"

"Yeah, another weird old law document was taken from the historical society in Farmingville," the chief said. He peered into my face. "Don't tell me you didn't know that."

I shook my head.

Chief McGinnis looked the tiniest bit satisfied. "Imagine me knowing something before Nancy Drew does," he said good-naturedly. "It was the same MO as the other thefts—no one around to see, the culprit left a mess all over the floor. And he took just one document: the original copy of a law stating that all married couples had to present the town of Farmingville with a potted hydrangea plant on the day of their wedding."

I laughed. "Why?" I asked.

"Apparently the founding fathers of Farmingville wanted the hydrangea to be the official town flower, but they lacked the funding to buy enough plants on their own."

"Did it work?" I asked him.

The chief shrugged. "You'll have to ask your friend Luther Eldridge about that," he said. "Now I really have to get over to the middle school. Nice to see you, Nancy."

I thought it was the first time I'd ever heard him say that and mean it. I got the feeling that it made Chief McGinnis's day to help me out with a case I'm working on. It doesn't happen very often.

When I got to Ms. Waters's house, I found her out in her garden, as usual.

"Hello, Nancy," she said when she saw me. She held up a lilac she had clipped for me to smell.

"That's beautiful," I told her.

Ms. Waters sighed and gazed over her garden. "It's hard to believe that this could be my last season in this house," she said sadly.

"I wish I could help more," I replied. "I've had no luck figuring out who took the document we need for you. The police did try to dust for fingerprints, but by the time they got there, we had already messed up most of the evidence. We had no idea that it was a crime scene when we walked in."

Ms. Waters nodded. "I can see why," she said. "I wouldn't think anyone in town would be interested in those old archives except for Luther and myself."

"I'm starting to think it's someone who's interested in the laws, not the actual documents," I told her. "Chief McGinnis said another old document was stolen a few towns over yesterday. This law was about hydrangeas. Add that to the pickle-eating law and the law about zoning, and you have a collection of strange laws."

"But stealing the papers they're written on doesn't mean you own the actual laws," Ms. Waters pointed out.

"I know," I said. "Still, some people like to collect things that are one of a kind, and these laws are certainly one of a kind!"

The old woman sighed. "If anyone can get to the bottom of this, it's you, Nancy," she said. "But I'm afraid it won't be in time to help me. The preliminary hearing is next week, and your father says that after that we'll know if the case is even worth fighting. It may just be a lost cause."

There wasn't much I could say to comfort her, and I left soon afterward feeling helpless. I headed straight for the airport—it was time for my third lesson with Frank Beltrano. I'd had the second one two days earlier, and it was even more fun than the first time. Frank had actually let me fly almost the whole time we were in the air. Today we were going to be working on takeoffs and landings. I knew it was a little early for me to be doing complicated things like landing the plane, but I hoped I would at least be able to take off once.

The airport was almost empty when I got there. Even Janice Mallory wasn't around. And neither was Frank. I checked my watch. He was late. The sun was already beginning to sink toward the horizon, and once again I was concerned that it would get dark during my lesson. Frank had been right on time for the second lesson, so I'd assumed his lateness the first time had been a fluke. But if that was the case, then where was he now?

He finally showed up almost half an hour late. "Hi, Nancy!" he called cheerfully. "Ready to learn how to take off?"

"Sure," I said. He didn't even seem to be aware that he was late. As I followed him out to the plane, I wondered if I'd accidentally come early. I opened my wallet and pulled out his business card. My father had written the dates and times of my lessons on the back. Sure enough, next to today's date he had scrawled *5:00 P.M.* It was after 5:30.

"Hop in," Frank said when we reached the Cessna. "We have a lot to do today."

He was so full of positive energy that it seemed

wrong to complain about his tardiness. I decided to mention it later, after the lesson.

When I was all strapped in, I assumed Frank would go over takeoff procedure with me. Instead, he did it all himself without even explaining what he was doing. We were in the air before I knew it.

"Will I take off the next time?" I asked. "I think I saw most of what you did."

Frank started, almost as if he'd forgotten I was there. "You're a good observer," he commented. "That's one of the best ways to learn."

I knew he was right. Still, I had really wanted to take off on my own. I was impatient to be able to do everything. "Why don't you walk me through the takeoff and I'll tell you what you're missing," Frank suggested.

"Okay," I agreed. "First, look at the runway to make sure no other planes are nearby or getting ready to land. Even if the tower says it's okay, I should check with my own eyes."

I tried to remember everything else the colonel had said about taking off.

"When I get to the end of the runway, I line up the nose with the center line. Then I gently and smoothly speed up and I go to full throttle. I keep checking the instruments."

I paused and looked at Frank. When he noticed me waiting, he smiled. "That's right," he said. "What next?"

"I put backward pressure on the control wheel," I said. "Again, moving very smoothly. That will lift the nose up to the correct angle for takeoff. After the plane lifts off, I slowly release my pressure on the control wheel so that I don't climb at too steep an angle." I pictured the way Colonel Lang took off, and the way Frank did it. They never jerked the wheel around at all—every movement was slow and controlled. "I should be aware that the controls feel tighter as the plane picks up speed," I said. "And if the plane starts bouncing, that means I need to apply more pressure to the control wheel to make the plane lift off. Once I'm off the ground, I need to be ready to adjust for crosswinds."

Frank didn't correct me much. In fact, he hardly said anything at all. He just listened, occasionally nodding or grunting an agreement with me. I wondered if he was really paying attention. Suddenly his cell phone rang.

"Whoops. Excuse me, Nancy," he said, pressing the Talk button.

I glanced outside. The red streaks of another beautiful sunset filled the sky to the west. It was still fun to be flying, but I hadn't had the controls even once during this lesson. And I thought it was a little rude of Frank to take phone calls while he was supposed to be teaching me. On our second lesson he hadn't even brought his cell phone along. That was how it should be every time.

Frank ended his phone call and turned to me with a grin. "Let's do a landing," he said. "There's a small airport up ahead—it's just a single runway, really. We'll land there, then take off again and head back to River Heights."

"Great!" I said. "Will I do the landing?"

"Oh, no," Frank replied quickly. "Landing is very tricky. I don't think you're ready for that yet. For now, you'll learn by watching."

But when he landed at the small airfield, he barely even explained what he was doing. I watched carefully, but without Frank explaining his actions, I was lost.

"I'm not sure I really followed that—," I started to say as we touched down.

"You'll get it eventually," Frank interrupted. He wasn't being rude really, but his voice was brusque. He taxied over to the small brick building that made up this tiny airport.

"I'll be right back, Nancy," he said, unbuckling his seat belt. "You can get out and stretch your legs if you want."

"No thanks," I answered as he climbed from the

plane. I couldn't hide my surprise. Where was he going? Maybe he had to check in at the control desk inside. I leaned my head back against the seat and watched the gorgeous red sunset. Soon enough it would be dark. We had to take off soon. Would Frank let me do it?

He returned very quickly, and I was surprised to see that he had a small package under his arm. It was a thin brown-paper-wrapped rectangle. Frank stuck it into his flight bag and strapped himself back in.

"Ready?" he asked.

"Sure," I replied. "Can I do the takeoff?"

He squinted into the gathering darkness. "It's getting late. You'd better let me do it," he said. "We don't want the gloom to throw you off."

He taxied quickly to the end of the runway.

"But there are no lines on this runway," I said. "How do you know where to line up the plane?"

"If you don't have a center line, pick a spot at the far end of the strip," Frank said. "Then you keep your eye on that as you take off. That will keep the plane moving in a straight line."

I watched carefully as Frank sped up, applied full throttle, and eased back on the control wheel. The takeoff was so smooth that I didn't even notice when we left the ground. I couldn't wait until it was my turn to try that.

By the time we landed back at the River Heights airport, it was almost completely dark. I felt a little irritated. Frank had let me have the controls once we were up in the air on the way back, but he had done all the takeoffs and landings himself. I didn't really feel I had learned much. I thought of the way Ned approached his lessons with Colonel Lang. Ned was patient, and he didn't mind not being in charge of the plane. Maybe I should try to be more like him, and take flying step by step. After all, I *had* learned about piloting a plane simply from watching what Frank did.

As I walked back to my car after the lesson, I was surprised to see a familiar plane parked outside the hangar. It was Colonel Lang's green-and-yellow Meridian. I took a quick look at the parking lot. Sure enough, there was the colonel's rental car. On a hunch I went back inside the hangar and took a good look around. No colonel. He wasn't in his car, either. Or his plane.

"Still, it's pretty clear that he's in town," I muttered to myself. The colonel's strange behavior bothered me for some reason. Why would he tell the Nickersons he was out of town when he wasn't?

I drove home past Ms. Waters's house. And that's when it struck me—the archive thefts had started only after Colonel Lang came to town! There was no reason to think he'd be involved in something like stealing old documents . . . but his car had been parked outside the antique shop for a long time the other day. Old legal documents counted as antiques, didn't they? Maybe the colonel stole the papers, then sold them to Mr. Berring, the antique dealer.

A little voice in my head told me that I was leaping to conclusions. I had no evidence that either the colonel or Mr. Berring were involved in anything illegal. But both of them had exhibited strange behavior lately, strange enough to draw my notice. I had a gut feeling that there was some connection between the two men. And my gut is usually right.

I called George. "Are you up for some sleuthing?" I asked when she picked up the phone.

"You bet," she answered. "What are we doing?"

"Staking out Colonel Lang," I told her.

"Isn't he a friend of Ned's father?" George asked. "Why do you want to stake him out?"

"I'm not really sure," I admitted. "But I've caught him in a lie, and I know he was involved in something shady back in Washington a long time ago. He and Mr. Nickerson hinted at it, but they never said outright what it was."

"And now he's lying to the Nickersons about where he is," George finished for me.

"Right. His car was parked near the antique shop for a long time the other day. Both he and Mr. Berring are new in town, and the document thefts didn't start until they got here. I have a hunch that there's a connection between them."

"Well, if there's one thing I've learned from being your friend, it's that even though your hunches are bizarre sometimes, we should listen," George told me. "I'll call Bess. We can take turns watching Mr. Berring's store until the colonel shows up."

"Thanks, George," I said. "You're the best!"

For the next two days, Bess, George, and I took turns parking along River Street to keep an eye on the antique store. Once or twice I spotted Colonel Lang's car, but I never saw him in person. I had to admit, he was pretty good at staying out of sight.

On the third day, I sat alone in my car, gazing at the door to Berring Antiques. I thought over everything I knew about the colonel. He was retired from the air force, and he'd known Ned's father in Washington, D.C. They'd both hinted that the colonel had been involved in a situation that Mr. Nickerson helped cover up. I realized that I barely knew anything about the man. I had been so charmed by his easygoing manners that I hadn't noticed how little information he gave out about himself. For all I knew, he'd been involved in illegal activities all his life.

Just as I was thinking this, my passenger-side door opened. And Colonel Lang got in.

10

A Revealing Conversation

"Hello, Nancy," the colonel said pleasantly as he settled himself in my car.

I was so surprised to see him that I just sat there and stared.

"Are you on a stakeout?" he asked. He nodded toward Berring Antiques across the street. "See anything interesting?"

What was I supposed to say? I'd only been watching the store in order to find the colonel, and here he was in my car! I decided to go with the truth. Well, *some* of the truth, anyway. "I haven't seen anything at all," I admitted.

"What are you looking for?" Colonel Lang asked.

I hesitated. I didn't want to tell him my suspicions about him and Mr. Berring. And besides, I wasn't entirely sure *what* I was looking for. I studied the colonel's face. He was smiling, but I still found it intimidating to have him in my car. Who knew what this man had been up to? I decided to take the offensive. "I thought you were out of town, Colonel," I said. "Ned and his family all think you're in Washington."

A flicker of amusement crossed his face. "I just got back," he replied.

"I've been seeing your car around all week," I told him. "And I saw your plane at the airport the other day."

Now the colonel looked surprised. "What were you doing at the airport?" he asked.

"What were *you* doing at the airport?" I countered. "You obviously weren't in D.C."

"No, I wasn't," he agreed. "I'm here on business that I can't really discuss."

"Why would you lie to the Nickersons?" I pressed.

"Because I don't want to get them involved," he said.

"Involved in what?" I asked.

"What do you think?" he replied.

I paused. He was asking me what I thought was going on with Mr. Berring, and the truth was that I didn't know for sure. I didn't even have that many clues. But if Colonel Lang was doing illegal business with the antique dealer, that meant he had to protect himself. If I told him that I suspected him of wrongdoing, it could put me in danger.

"I think Mr. Berring may be involved in selling stolen historical documents," I said. That was true, and it didn't imply that I thought the colonel was the one supplying those stolen documents.

"Really?" Colonel Lang sounded surprised.

"Why?" I asked him. "What do you think?"

He looked at me for a moment as if he'd never seen me before. "You really are quite the detective, aren't you?" he said, almost to himself.

"Yes, I am," I replied. I was relieved that my voice sounded normal, since my heart was pounding. If Colonel Lang really was involved in Mr. Berring's scheme, would he try to keep me quiet somehow?

"What makes you think Berring is selling stolen merchandise?" he asked.

"A hunch mostly," I admitted. "Someone has been stealing old documents from archives around the county, and Berring Antiques is new in town. The thefts only started after he got here."

Colonel Lang nodded. "I can see why you would draw that conclusion," he said. "These documents are antiques, and he sells antiques."

"Do you know something more about it?" I asked boldly.

"Why would I?" the colonel replied.

"Because I have a hunch about you, too," I admitted. "You've been lying to the Nickersons, and you've been staking out the antique shop."

"You noticed that, huh?" He chuckled.

"Do you know Mr. Berring?" I asked.

"In a sense," he said. "But he doesn't know me."

"What does that mean?" I asked.

In response the colonel reached into the inside pocket of his jacket and pulled out a large, flat leather wallet. He handed it to me.

I opened the wallet to find an FBI badge with Colonel Lang's name and photo.

"FBI?" I cried. "You're an FBI agent?"

"That's right," he said, taking the badge back. "Surprised?"

"Yes," I said truthfully. What I didn't say out loud was how relieved I also was. Here I'd been thinking that one of Mr. Nickerson's oldest friends was some kind of thief! I was certainly glad to know he wasn't here for any illegal reasons. But the fact that he was an FBI agent meant that he *was* here for a reason. "You're investigating Mr. Berring, aren't you?" I asked.

"Yes, I am," the colonel replied. "I've been investigating him for some time, in fact. He relocated here after his last scheme fell apart. Of course, he used a different name then."

"I knew it," I said. "There was just something about his behavior that made me suspicious. And then when the archive break-ins began, somehow it made me think of him."

"The archives are the least of his crimes," the colonel said. "In fact I'm not even sure he's the one stealing the documents. We have reason to believe that he's involved in the smuggling of not only historical papers, but also valuable artworks."

"Why hasn't he been arrested?" I asked.

"We believe he's a small part of a larger smuggling ring," Colonel Lang explained. "We're not sure how he's receiving the pieces, or how he ships them to his clients."

"So you don't want to arrest him until you can identify the whole group," I said.

The colonel smiled. "You got it," he replied. "I must say, I'm impressed with you, Nancy. You almost blew my cover! No one else realized that I was connected to Mr. Berring in any way."

"I just notice things," I told him. "For instance, I first noticed Mr. Berring at the airport when we were there for our first lesson with you. He seemed so angry. It stuck in my mind. That's why I noticed him when he was driving around and around on River Street. It almost seemed as if he was looking for someone."

"I didn't see that," the colonel replied. "Did you find out who he was looking for?"

I shook my head. "He may have been looking for a parking spot for all I know," I admitted. "But now that you've told me he's a smuggler, I think he was probably looking for his contact."

Colonel Lang nodded thoughtfully. "I did notice him at the airport," he said slowly. "I wondered what he was doing there."

"He was there to yell at somebody," I told him. "But I never found out what it was about."

"Thanks for the info, Nancy," Colonel Lang said, putting his badge back in his pocket. "But now that you know what's going on, I'd like you to drop your investigation."

"Why?" I asked. I was still hoping to find the thief so that I could recover the original zoning law document to help Ms. Waters.

"Because the people in this smuggling ring are professional criminals," Colonel Lang said. "That means that anyone who finds out about them will be in danger. These people will resort to violence to avoid being caught." He held my eye for a moment, a serious expression on his craggy face. "It's too dangerous for you, Nancy. Promise me you'll stay out of it."

I never like being told to drop a case. But when an FBI agent gives you a direct order, you'd better do as you're told. "Okay," I said reluctantly.

"Good. But when this is all done, I'll give you your own flying lesson to thank you for your help," he said.

"I may not need it," I said with a smile. "I'm already taking lessons with Frank Beltrano."

"Really? Good for you!" Colonel Lang looked pleased.

"Flying with you and Ned inspired me," I added.

"Well, I'm glad you enjoyed it." The colonel opened the car door. "Have fun flying."

"Thanks," I called as he closed the door and headed off down the sidewalk. I glanced up at Berring Antiques. It was frustrating to know that Mr. Berring might be in possession of the original copy of the zoning law that could save Ms. Waters's home. If only I could go in there and search for it. . . .

I turned on the car and prepared to pull out of my parking space. Colonel Lang had told me to stay out of it. So I would.

11

A Lesson in Disaster

I was glad to have a flying lesson that afternoon to take my mind off the situation with Colonel Lang and the smuggling ring. I knew the FBI would solve their case, but it could take weeks, or even months. That would be way too late to help Evaline Waters. Plus, I still wished I could assist in the investigation. I hated dropping the case before it was solved. In fact, I had never done that before.

On the way to the airport I called Bess and George to tell them that our stakeout of Berring Antiques was over. I didn't want to reveal that Colonel Lang was FBI, so I simply told them I had made a mistake about him and that I no longer suspected him. I knew they were curious, but they were just going to have to wait to hear the whole story.

I also called Ned to invite him along on my flying lesson, but his mother said he was studying at the university library. I felt a little relieved—I was nervous that I hadn't told him yet about my lessons. And the more time that went by without my telling him, the more I felt as if I was hiding something from him. Ugh. I promised myself that the next day I'd sit down with him and explain the whole thing.

When I walked into the hangar, I half expected to find that Frank was late again. But instead he was sitting on his counter reading a magazine. As soon as he saw me, he hopped off. "Let's get going," he said, putting on his sunglasses.

I felt a bounce in my step as I followed him out to the plane. The lesson was starting on time, it was a beautiful sunny day, and I felt confident in my flying abilities. "Do you think I can take off today?" I asked. "I feel ready."

Frank looked me up and down. "I don't see why not," he said. "I'll take off first, so we can go through the steps slowly. Then we'll land, and you can take off the second time."

"Great!" I replied. It was strange how Frank's teaching style changed so much from one lesson to the next. We strapped ourselves into our seats, then I radioed the tower for permission to take off. Frank slowly went through the entire process, explaining each move he made.

By the time we were airborne, I had memorized the whole procedure. "Since I only have one more lesson after this one, do you think I could practice taking off today and then practice landing on Friday?" I asked.

Frank glanced at me in surprise. "Our next lesson is Monday," he corrected me.

"I don't think so," I said. "I'm pretty sure it's on Friday. Let me look." Since Frank was still at the controls, I leaned over the side of my seat and pulled my bag from the mesh compartment under the chair. I still had the business card that Dad had written my lesson schedule on. I stuck my hand into the bag and felt around for the small piece of stiff paper. Bess is always telling me to organize my bag better, but I never find the time to do it.

Finally I felt the business card. I pulled it out and checked the dates Dad had inked on the back. "Yeah, it's Friday," I said.

"Huh. I guess I remembered wrong." Frank shot me a smile. "Friday it is."

"Can I land the plane on Friday?" I asked.

"We'll see," he replied. "Landing is tricky."

While he spoke I turned his card over in my hand and idly studied the front of it. I had never really looked at the printed side before. It featured a cute little cartoon of Frank in the Cessna, along with his name and phone number. I grinned when I saw the number.

"Your phone number is close to my boyfriend's," I told him. "Yours is five-five-five, four-three-seven-oh. His is four-three-four-oh. You have to picture the dial pad. The four is just above the seven. It's an easy dialing error. I bet you two get each other's wrong numbers all the time!"

As the words left my mouth, I felt realization dawn. The strange caller Ned's father had told me about—that was someone trying to call Frank Beltrano. Ned's father *had* been getting Frank's wrong numbers. And as soon as I realized that, all the other bits and pieces of suspicion I'd been feeling began to make sense. Mr. Nickerson's mystery caller always said there was a package delivery that night. But that message was really meant to tell Frank that there was a delivery.

I was willing to bet that the call he'd gotten during our last lesson was one of those very phone calls—after he'd received it, he landed at the other airport and picked up a package. He'd gotten two calls during our lessons, now that I thought about it. And both times it had been at sunset. Harold Safer's story about sailors and sunsets filled my mind. What had he said? *Red sky at night, sailors' delight . . .* When the sunset showed a red sky, it meant the weather would be clear for a little while.

And clear weather meant easy flying. Frank could fly out during a clear night to pick up one of his mysterious packages. But why all the secrecy about package delivery? Why would he need to go at night?

I knew the answer immediately. Frank wasn't really a flight instructor—that was just his cover. He was a smuggler! He was the one Colonel Lang was looking for. Now I understood why Mr. Berring had been at the airport that day: He was there to yell at Frank. Mr. Nickerson had gotten one of the wrong-number calls the night before, which meant that Frank hadn't gotten the call meant for him. He'd probably missed his cue to go and pick up one of the stolen documents or a piece of artwork. Mr. Berring had come to the airport to find out why—and he'd been pretty angry about it. No wonder Frank hadn't wanted to admit to me that he knew Mr. Berring!

I pictured the thin, rectangular package Frank had picked up during our last lesson. Could that have been the very document my friends and I were looking for—the one that would help Ms. Waters? I felt sick just thinking about it. I had been with him while he was transporting stolen goods. I had participated in the smuggling ring!

"Why so quiet, Nancy?" Frank asked. "Thinking about your takeoff? We're still about five minutes from the airport."

I just stared at him. I didn't know what to say.

"I'll land there, and then you can take off again," he told me.

"Okay," I whispered. Now I had to figure out how to get out of the plane when we landed so that I could notify the authorities. Maybe I could pretend to be sick. . . .

He squinted at me. "Are you sure you're okay?" he asked. Suddenly he reached for my arm. I gasped and pulled away. Surprised, he jerked back. His elbow hit the control wheel and knocked it forward. Frank's eyes met mine for a brief moment, and then the plane went into a steep dive.

It happened so quickly that Frank was taken by surprise. He fell forward, his loosened seat belt not stopping him. His head smacked against the control panel with a dull thud. Without thinking, I grabbed the control wheel and yanked it up. The plane pulled up so quickly that Frank tumbled backward against his seat. His head lolled to the side. He was unconscious.

There was no one to land the plane!

12

A Dangerous Landing

"Frank!" I yelled, gripping the control wheel tightly. "Frank, wake up!" I pried one hand off the wheel and swatted at him, hitting him as hard as I could without jostling the wheel.

It was no use. Frank didn't even twitch a muscle. He must've hit his head harder than I thought.

"Okay, Nancy, calm down," I told myself. But it was hard. I was alone in a plane with only three lessons under my belt. When I glanced down at the ground rushing by, I felt sick to my stomach. I had never been so afraid in my life.

Luckily I had some experience in dangerous situations. Never as bad as this, but I'd felt threatened before on my cases. The most important thing was to keep a clear head. Remembering this, I took a deep breath.

"I'm in control, and I know how to keep us in the air flying in a straight line," I said aloud. "So I just need to keep doing what I'm doing while I get help."

Talking to myself made me feel more in control. I forced myself to look at the bright side: At least I wasn't in any danger from Frank the Smuggler. For now, I could concentrate on flying without having to worry about him. I held the wheel steady and reached for the radio. With one thumb, I flipped the switch to turn it on.

What should I say? "Mayday," I whispered into the microphone. That's what they always say in movies. I figured maybe it would work. I cleared my throat and spoke louder. "Mayday, mayday. Cessna Skyhawk in need of assistance."

I released the Talk button and waited for someone—anyone—to answer. For a moment there was nothing but a crackling sound. Then a woman's voice came over the airwaves.

"Copy, Skyhawk. Is that you, Nancy?"

"Janice?" I cried. I was thrilled to hear the manager's voice. "I need help," I said in a rush. "Frank's been knocked unconscious and I have to land the plane."

There was silence on the other end. Then Janice said, "I'm not a pilot, Nancy." Her voice shook. "I don't know how to land a plane."

My heart stopped. The people on the ground were my only hope. If they couldn't help, what would I do?

"I'm going to try to find someone," Janice said. She sounded as frightened as I felt. "Just keep flying, okay?"

"Okay," I said numbly. I glanced over at Frank. He was still out.

After what felt like forever, the radio crackled again. "Nancy?" cried a deep male voice. "It's Colonel Lang."

When I heard him, relief washed over me. The colonel would get me down safely, I just knew it. "I'm here," I said. "What should I do?"

"The first thing is to stay calm," he said. "I'm in the tower and I can see you on radar."

"Good," I said. "I'm flying toward the airport. Frank was heading back that way before he got knocked out."

"Did something happen?" the colonel asked. "Why is he unconscious?"

I felt a little weird saying this over the radio, but I had no choice. "I realized that Frank was the smuggler you're looking for. He noticed that I was acting strange and he reached out for me. I panicked and jumped, then he hit the wheel and the plane started to go into a dive. That's when his head hit the control panel."

"I see," Colonel Lang said, sounding dazed.

"Colonel, I can see the airport now," I told him. "How do I get down?"

"Okay, Nancy, listen carefully," he said. "I'll talk you in. Do you understand?"

"Yes," I told him.

"You're not going to start your landing until you're pretty low," he said. "About twenty feet. That's roughly the height of the hangar roof. Okay?"

"Okay," I said. I could see the hangar in the distance. "Should I start lowering the plane now?"

"Yes, very gently," said the colonel.

I pressed the control wheel down ever so slightly, and the nose of the plane eased downward.

"Now, Nancy, in order to land the plane, you're going to do something called a power-off stall," the colonel said.

That didn't sound very safe! "I'm going to stall on purpose?" I asked doubtfully.

"It's okay; it's a normal way to land," he said soothingly. "It means you'll be going as slow as possible when you touch down."

That sounded good. "Okay," I said.

"As you land, don't watch the ground in front of you," he said. "It will distort your depth perception."

I felt a trickle of sweat on my brow as I tried to

process what he was saying. "Don't look forward?" I asked. I was looking over the nose of the plane right now.

"No," he said. "Because when you land, you're going to lift the nose up. And then you won't be able to see the ground over the top of it."

That made sense. "But then where should I look?" I asked.

"Look to the left," he instructed me. "Past the left side of the nose and to the ground in front of it."

I tried looking where he said, and I realized I got a much better idea of how far down the ground really was when I did it this way. Looking over the top had given me the impression that I was moving much faster than I really was. "Okay, I get it," I told him. I didn't feel nervous anymore—I was too busy concentrating on doing what the colonel said.

"You're at the right height now," he said. "You're going to begin the stall. Ready?"

"Yes," I said. "What should I do?"

"Ease back on the wheel," he said. "But make sure you do it gradually. If you pull too hard, the plane will shoot back up."

"Got it," I said, gently pulling back on the wheel. The plane's nose tilted up into the air. I forced myself to keep focused on what I was doing, even though a part of me wanted to panic. I remembered that I was supposed to stall, that it was normal.

"Just keep that gentle pressure on the wheel, Nancy," Colonel Lang said. "You're doing great. We want to keep the nose tilted up."

I nodded, even though he couldn't see me. I kept my eyes glued to the ground outside the left window of the plane. As I got lower and lower, it got harder to keep the nose up. I held on tightly to the wheel and kept pulling back.

Suddenly I felt a bump, then another.

"Your back wheels are down!" the colonel cried excitedly. "Keep the nose in the air. It will help slow you down."

I kept pulling back on the wheel until he told me to ease off. Slowly the front of the plane came down and gently touched the runway. I applied the brakes, and the plane gradually slowed. Finally it stopped.

I had done it! I was down!

Then everything happened at once. I noticed flashing lights on the runway. The door opened and a police officer stuck her head in. She helped me out while a paramedic climbed into the plane to tend to Frank. When my feet touched the ground, my knees buckled a little. I was so relieved!

"Nancy!" My father came running from the hangar and threw his arms around me.

"Dad? What are you doing here?" I asked.

"I asked Janice to call him when we heard what was going on," said a deep voice from behind. I turned to see Colonel Lang with a big grin on his face.

"Colonel! Thank you so much!" I cried.

"You did all the hard work," he said. "Most people would have panicked in your situation, but you kept your cool. I can see why your dad is so proud of you."

Dad gave my shoulders a squeeze. "You were just touching down when I got here," he told me. "I'm glad I missed most of it. You may have kept your cool, but I doubt that I could have! Thank goodness you were at the airport, Colonel."

I frowned. "Why *were* you at the airport?" I asked.

"I was worried about you," the colonel replied. "We had just caught Berring with a stolen etching in his possession, and he confessed to everything . . . including his connection to Frank Beltrano. I guess you figured that out too."

"Yeah, at the worst possible time!" I joked. Now that I was safely back on the ground, the events of the last half hour were starting to feel like a dream.

"Well, at least you're safe now," Dad said. "My heart is still pounding."

"Actually, I was hoping to land at the next lesson," I said. "I guess I got what I wanted a little early."

The paramedics helped Frank Beltrano from the plane. He was conscious now, and looking confused. "I'd better go," the colonel said. "We're taking Beltrano into custody. He should be able to tell us the names of the rest of the operation."

I didn't bother to watch Frank being arrested. Dad and I turned and walked slowly toward the parking lot. We passed Chief McGinnis, who was heading for the planes.

"I guess you cracked your stolen documents case, Nancy," he said. "Are you all right?"

I nodded. "I'm fine, thanks, Chief."

He glanced at my father. "I should've known she'd get to the bottom of this," he said. "We had no idea a few archive thefts could be such a big deal." He sounded a little miffed.

"Well, how could you know we would find a major smuggling ring?" I said, trying to make him feel better. I don't think it worked though. He just raised his eyebrows.

"I'm going to get Nancy home," Dad said, leading me away.

"Bye, Chief!" I called. Since Dad had caught a ride to the airport with a friend, he drove us home in my car. And that was fine by me. I didn't want to be behind the wheel of anything—car or plane—for a long time!

But as we drove past Ms. Waters's house, I realized with a start that we might be able to find the zoning law document now. "Dad," I said, "do you think Colonel Lang could help us recover the stolen document from the university archive?"

Dad furrowed his brow. "I doubt it," he said slowly. "Even if the FBI has found all the stolen items, they would be considered evidence. We wouldn't be allowed to have access to them."

"But we wouldn't need to bring the actual document into court, would we?" I asked. "I mean, you and Mr. Shannon and the judge could all go and read the document while it's still in FBI custody, and then you could use it in the case."

"Are you a lawyer now too?" Dad teased. "It's possible that we could do that, but it would be up to the judge. And we don't even know if the colonel has found that particular stolen document."

"I bet Colonel Lang would help me find out," I said. "I'm the one who alerted him to the connection between Mr. Berring and Frank Beltrano. He owes me one."

Dad turned the car into our driveway. "The colonel helped you land that plane. I think *you* owe *him* one."

He was right. But I still thought Colonel Lang might be willing to help me one more time. As Dad parked, I noticed Hannah rushing out the front door with a worried look on her face. I climbed out of the car and got ready for a bear hug, Gruen-style.

"Nancy, thank goodness you're all right!" Hannah cried, throwing her arms around me. "I knew you were crazy to be flying around in little planes like that. Promise me you'll never do it again."

"Well, I don't know, Hannah," I said. "I'll have to think about it." There was one thing I didn't have to think about though—finishing the Evaline Waters case. Colonel Lang may have wrapped up his smuggling case, but I hadn't wrapped up my case yet. And I was going to, no matter what.

13

An Informative Conversation

The next morning I called Ned before he had even finished his breakfast. "I need your help," I told him. "I have to ask Colonel Lang for a favor."

Ned hesitated. "I think you're closer to the colonel now than I am," he said. "The story of your spectacular landing is all over my dad's paper this morning."

There was a strange sound in his voice, and I suddenly realized that I'd never told Ned about my flying lessons! He'd had to find out what I was up to by reading a newspaper article.

"Oh, Ned, I'm so sorry!" I cried. "I've been meaning to tell you all this past week! I loved flying with you and the colonel so much that I asked my father for lessons with Frank Beltrano."

"Why didn't you tell me?" Ned asked.

I bit my lip. Why *hadn't* I told him? "I guess I thought you might feel uncomfortable with it," I admitted. "Because taking flying lessons was your idea. And I was so excited about it, but you . . ."

"I wasn't," Ned finished for me.

"Well, no," I said. "I was impatient for more time in the air, but when the colonel said he was going away for a while, you actually seemed relieved."

"That's because I *was* relieved," Ned said. "Flying terrifies me!"

"What?" I cried. Ned Nickerson *terrified*? I couldn't imagine such a thing. Ned was the bravest person I knew.

"I don't mind flying in a jet with an experienced pilot and copilot," Ned said. "But up in that little plane, with only my dad's friend at the controls . . . it scared me."

"Why did you ask Colonel Lang for lessons, then?" I asked.

"I was kidding," Ned replied, abashed. "I never thought he'd take me seriously."

I couldn't help smiling. "But then when he said yes, you felt it would be rude not to take him up on his generous offer to teach you to fly," I guessed.

"You know me, polite to a fault," Ned answered.

His voice was back to normal now, and I knew everything was okay between us.

"You should have told me you were afraid," I said.

"I didn't want to ruin your fun," Ned replied. "I knew you weren't scared at all."

"I was plenty scared yesterday," I admitted.

"I'll bet. Are you okay?" Ned asked gently.

"I'm okay," I told him. "Though I wouldn't be if Colonel Lang hadn't been there."

"So what's the favor you need to ask him?"

Evaline Waters and her situation came rushing back into my mind. "I want him to let me see a piece of evidence from the smuggling ring. A stolen document."

"The zoning law for Ms. Waters's lawsuit?" Ned guessed.

"That's right," I said. "But I don't know if the FBI has recovered that document yet. And I don't even know where Colonel Lang is staying, so I can't ask him!"

"Well, that's easy," Ned said. "He's staying here with us. Come on over."

I was out of my chair before he even finished speaking. "I'll be right there!" I said.

When I reached the Nickerson house, Colonel Lang was out on the front lawn, playing ball with

Ned and his dad. He didn't look anything like an air force colonel or an FBI agent. He just looked like an overgrown boy, diving to make a great catch. When he saw me, he tossed the football my way. I caught it easily.

The colonel grinned. "Is there anything she can't do?" he asked Ned.

"Not that I know of," Ned said, ruffling my hair.

"Well, there is *one* thing," I said. "I can't get into locked FBI evidence rooms."

Mr. Nickerson laughed. "She's also not good at beating around the bush," he told his old friend. "Nancy always says just what she means."

I blushed. I guess I hadn't been very subtle. I just wanted Ms. Waters to stop worrying as soon as possible!

"You'd like to see some of the evidence from the smuggling case?" Colonel Lang asked.

I nodded. "There's an old law I need to see to help out a friend. It's so old that there's only one written copy of it in existence."

"And it was stolen," the colonel guessed.

"Yes. Have you recovered all the stolen goods?" I asked.

He shook his head. "We've found the central members of the smuggling ring, but we haven't located all their buyers yet. They're spread out all over the country, if not the world. Plus, they cover their tracks—they're trafficking in stolen goods, so they make themselves hard to find."

My heart sank. I'd been hoping he could just take me to see the stolen documents right away. "I hadn't thought of it that way," I said. "It will probably take months to find them all."

"It will," he replied. His voice was grave, but there was a twinkle in his eye. "However," he went on, "there is one thing I can tell you, sleuth to sleuth."

"Yes?" I prompted.

"When I talked to you in your car, you mentioned that the local archive thefts hadn't started until after Berring moved to town," the colonel said.

"That's right," I said.

"Well, that got me thinking," Colonel Lang said. "Why would Berring come here to River Heights to restart his life of crime? It's not a major hub for the type of art he usually smuggled."

I thought it over. "Because there was something here that he wanted?" I guessed.

"Exactly," Colonel Lang replied. "He wanted your historical documents!"

Ned looked doubtful. "Why?" he asked. "The things that were stolen weren't valuable. Even the police weren't very interested in them."

"That's true," Mr. Nickerson put in. "But the fact that they were stolen means they must have been valuable to someone."

"So Mr. Berring found a buyer who was interested in old laws," I said, thinking it through. "Maybe it was one of his big art customers, or someone with lots of money to spend. Mr. Berring thought it was worth the trouble to steal those historical documents for his buyer."

"It wasn't a hard job," Colonel Lang said. "As you know, the archives weren't well guarded, and no one really cared that obscure documents were disappearing. In fact, I don't think anyone even noticed the pattern of thefts until you came along."

"How many documents were stolen?" Mr. Nickerson asked.

"Twenty-three, from archives in River Heights and six neighboring towns," the colonel revealed.

I gasped. "Twenty-three!"

Colonel Lang nodded. "It was Berring's downfall. The thefts were so simple that he did the dirty work himself."

"You mean he didn't hire anyone to steal the documents? It was actually Mr. Berring who went into the archives and took the papers?" I asked. I wondered how that could have been the man's downfall. And suddenly it came to me! "So you had hard evidence of Mr. Berring committing a crime," I said. "You were able to tie him to the crime scenes—the archives."

"Yes, thanks to you," Colonel Lang said. "Yesterday while you were taking your flying lesson, we had FBI teams visit the county archive. The local police hadn't found any fingerprints, but we have more sophisticated equipment. We located one fingerprint on the bottom of a file folder that had been tossed on the floor. It matched Berring's fingerprint."

"And then what?" I asked. I couldn't believe my information had been so instrumental in bringing down an international smuggler!

"And then I was able to threaten him with jail time for breaking and entering unless he cooperated with our investigation," Colonel Lang said. "Once I did that, Berring was happy to snitch on his colleagues."

"Including Frank Beltrano," I said. Something still didn't add up. "But why was Mr. Berring's buyer so interested in old laws from this county?" I asked. "Why did he have to come to River Heights?"

"Good question," Mr. Nickerson put in. "I expect that every town has its share of strange old laws."

"That's the best part," Colonel Lang said. "This buyer wanted obscure *local* laws."

"You mean the buyer is from around here?" I asked excitedly. "From this county?"

"According to Berring, this was the only county the buyer was interested in," the colonel replied. "But they always communicated via e-mail. Berring swears he doesn't know the buyer's identity."

"That's okay," I said. "Because I have a pretty good idea who it is!"

14

Finding the Culprit

I knocked on the door of Kaylin Marshall's office. Ned and Colonel Lang stood right behind me.

"I hope you're sure about this, Nancy," Colonel Lang said. "I'd hate to accuse an innocent person."

"That's why we're here," I told him. "To find out for sure."

The door creaked open to reveal Kaylin. "Nancy, Ned, hi," she said, surprised. She glanced at Colonel Lang. "What can I do for you guys?"

"You said we could come to you for information," I told her. "Any public information, right?"

"Of course," Kaylin said. "Come on in. Sorry the office is a mess."

"Where's your boss?" Ned asked. "Mr. Williams?"

"Out demonstrating," Kaylin replied. "It's lunch hour."

I took a seat at Kaylin's desk and smiled at her. "He really goes out every day, huh?"

"Like clockwork," she said.

"And do you always know where he is?" I pressed. "Which town hall he's picketing?"

Kaylin frowned. "Well, no," she said. "I don't really care that much, actually. I get more work done when he's not here. He's always talking on and on about archive security when he's in the office. I'm just happy he's gone for an hour every day."

I exchanged a glance with Colonel Lang. "So Mr. Williams could actually be running a private errand—for instance, picking up a stolen document—during lunch hour?" Colonel Lang asked.

Kaylin looked surprised. "I—I suppose so. Nobody pays much attention to Mr. Williams. He's sort of a local joke."

I smiled. "Kaylin, is Mr. Williams's address a matter of public record?"

"Sure," she said. "Why?"

"Because we'd like to pay him a little visit," I said. "We want to see what kind of historical documents he has 'archived' at his house."

Kaylin scrawled the address for Felix Williams on a

piece of note paper, and Colonel Lang drove us straight there. We found Mr. Williams just locking up.

The colonel flashed his FBI badge. "Would you mind if we took a look inside?" he asked.

Felix Williams turned red from his pudgy, sandal-clad feet to the top of his bald head. "I—I'm on my way back to work," he stammered. "I just came home for lunch."

"Weren't you out protesting today?" I asked.

Mr. Williams just gaped at me.

"Are you sure I can't just take a peek inside?" Colonel Lang asked. "We've just broken a smuggling ring, and we're looking for their stolen merchandise. There would be a very severe penalty for anyone who tried to hide their involvement with the smugglers."

Mr. Williams's mouth dropped open.

"It's really in your best interest to tell us what you know," I told him.

"I'm sorry!" he burst out. "I didn't mean any harm! There were all these fascinating old documents and nobody was paying attention to their safety! I thought they would be lost forever in those musty, ill-kept archives!"

"So you paid to have someone steal them?" Ned asked.

Mr. Williams looked him up and down. "Well, I couldn't steal them myself," he retorted. "I'm not a criminal."

Colonel Lang stepped forward. "Hiring someone to commit a crime is also a crime," he pointed out.

"How can it be a crime to try to protect these whimsical old laws?" the red-faced man protested. "No one else even knows they exist!"

"You could have organized the archives better to ensure the safekeeping of the historical documents," I said. "Or you could have made sure the wording of the old laws was transferred onto the county computer systems. That way they wouldn't have been lost."

"Computers!" Mr. Williams said contemptuously. "What's a computer file compared to a two-hundred-year-old piece of parchment? That's history, young lady."

I didn't say anything. I was just glad George wasn't here to argue with him about the virtues of computers.

"I'm afraid that you've committed a crime, Mr. Williams, no matter how good your motives were," said Colonel Lang. "I'm placing you under arrest."

While the colonel read Mr. Williams his rights, I pulled out my cell phone and called Dad. He and

Mr. Shannon would have to get down here immediately in order to see the original copy of the zoning law that affected Ms. Waters's property.

Soon enough the police appeared to take Felix Williams into custody, followed by Dad in the passenger seat of Mr. Shannon's car. It always surprised me how friendly they could be, considering that they were usually on opposite sides of a lawsuit.

"Colonel, do you mind if we look for the legal document we need?" I asked. "We won't touch a thing. We just need to read it."

"Okay, but I'll need to be there at all times," Colonel Lang replied. "And only the concerned parties can come in—just the lawyers."

I felt a prick of disappointment. It would be nice to see that piece of paper after all I'd done to find it. But I knew my father would take care of everything. I nodded.

"I'm not guaranteeing that this is legally binding, Carson," Mr. Shannon said cheerfully.

"I know. We're just going to see what it says," Dad replied. The two men followed Colonel Lang inside. Ned and I stayed on the front porch, watching the county police drive off with Mr. Williams. For a moment there was silence. Then Dad and Mr. Shannon came racing out the door.

"Get your own ride back, Carson!" yelled Mr. Shannon. He sprinted toward his car.

Dad turned to me. "Who drove here?" he cried.

"Colonel Lang," I answered. "What's going on, Dad?"

The colonel came running out of the house. "I can't leave the crime scene until the FBI investigators get here," he said quickly. He fished his keys out of his jacket pocket and tossed them to Ned. "Take my car."

Dad grabbed my arm and pulled me to the car. Ned jumped in the driver's seat and turned the key in the ignition.

"Head for Ms. Waters's place," Dad commanded. Ned hit the gas and took off toward the retired librarian's house.

"What's happening?" I demanded from my place in the backseat.

"The law," Dad gasped, breathing hard. "It says that in a land dispute without proper documentation, whichever party reaches the town courthouse first can lay claim."

"What?" I cried. "That's ridiculous. What kind of way is that to settle a dispute?"

"It's a law from back when there were only about a hundred people in River Heights," Ned said, never taking his eyes from the road.

"Evaline needs to get to the courthouse and say, 'The land is mine,' three times before someone from Rackham Industries does," Dad added.

I could hardly believe my ears. But it made a strange kind of sense. Felix Williams had been mostly interested in oddball laws, and this one certainly qualified.

When we reached Ms. Waters's house, I leaped from the car and ran to her garden. Sure enough, she was there pulling up weeds. "Come on!" I yelled. "Get in the car if you want to save your land!"

Ms. Waters can run fast for an elderly lady. She almost beat me to the car.

Ned peeled out and drove as fast as the speed limit allowed all the way to the courthouse. On the way, I filled Ms. Waters in on what she had to say to the judge. When we pulled up in front of the stately brick building, she didn't even wait for Ned to stop the car. She just leaped out and ran up the steps. After she disappeared inside, I saw Mr. Shannon pull up with the head of Rackham Industries. Dad went over to meet them, but I didn't even bother following them into the courthouse. There was no way they would be able to catch up with Ms. Waters—she had too much of a head start.

I looked at Ned. Both of us were still breathing

hard from the stress of our race to the courthouse. He met my eye, and we burst out laughing.

"I guess Ms. Waters will keep her house after all," I said happily.

"Another victory for Nancy Drew, supersleuth," he teased. All I could do was grin.

A few days later I visited Evaline Waters with Bess and George. As soon as she had made her claim with the judge, Rackham Industries had dropped their suit against Ms. Waters. Mr. Shannon had seen the wording of the old law, and he knew my father would win in court if that law was brought up. Ms. Waters's home was safe. Now Dad was filing papers to get her a new copy of the deed to the property.

When we got there, she gave us each a bouquet of clipped flowers from her garden.

"These are beautiful!" Bess cried, burying her face in the fragrant blooms. George sneezed.

"You girls have saved my home!" Ms. Waters said gratefully. "You can have as many flowers as you want!"

"It was really Nancy's doing," George said. "She's the one who figured out the smuggling ring."

"And George is the one who figured out there was an old law to protect you in the first place," I pointed out. "It was teamwork."

"I still don't understand how that Mr. Berring actually stole the documents from the archives," Ms. Waters said.

"He made a full confession," Bess reported. "He would go into the archives, hide the documents in his backpack, and make a mess to throw police off the trail for a little while."

"He had someone else who stole artwork from galleries and museums," I added. "He didn't want to get caught doing that."

Ms. Waters made a tsking sound. "Artwork I can understand," she said, "because it's valuable. But why would anyone want those silly old legal documents?"

"That was a recent addition to Mr. Berring's business," George said. "Mr. Williams had been on a crusade all his life to save those oddball parchments. Apparently he'd saved up for years to have enough money to pay for their theft."

"In fact, he'd already bought almost thirty old legal documents from Mr. Berring," I added. "Laws from all over the county. These documents were so obscure that nobody noticed they were being stolen in bulk."

"Until Nancy Drew came along," Bess teased.

My cheeks grew hot. "No, until Ms. Waters's case

came along," I corrected her. "That's why we started looking for old documents."

"Then I'm glad I could help!" Ms. Waters said. "But I'm sorry it put you in such a dangerous situation, Nancy. I get chills just thinking of you having to land that plane all alone."

"It was pretty scary," I agreed. "At first I thought I'd never fly again. But Colonel Lang said I needed to get back on the horse."

"Don't you mean get back in the pilot's seat?" Bess asked.

"Yup," I said. "I'm going up this afternoon!"

When I got to the airport later, I spotted Frank Beltrano's Cessna under a tarp. No one would be using that for a while. I made my way to the green-and-yellow Piper Meridian. Colonel Lang was already there, and so was Ned.

"Hi, guys," I called.

"Hey, Nance," Ned said, giving me a kiss. "Ready to fly?"

"You bet," I replied.

As Colonel Lang did the flight precheck of the plane, I pulled Ned aside. "Are you sure you want to come along on my lesson?" I asked. "I know flying makes you nervous."

"Flying with me at the controls makes me nervous,"

Ned said. "But I'd trust you to pilot any plane in the world after your spectacular first landing!"

"I'll second that," Colonel Lang said, coming around the plane. "Are you ready for your next lesson, Nancy?"

"Absolutely," I said, squeezing my boyfriend's hand. "Let's fly!"

Have you read all of the Alice Books?

❑ THE AGONY OF ALICE
Atheneum Books for Young Readers
0-689-31143-5
Aladdin Paperbacks 0-689-81672-3

❑ ALICE IN RAPTURE, SORT OF
Atheneum Books for Young Readers
0-689-31466-3
Aladdin Paperbacks 0-689-81687-1

❑ RELUCTANTLY ALICE
Atheneum Books for Young Readers
0-689-31681-X

❑ ALL BUT ALICE
Atheneum Books for Young Readers
0-689-31773-5

❑ ALICE IN APRIL
Atheneum Books for Young Readers
0-689-31805-7

❑ ALICE IN-BETWEEN
Atheneum Books for Young Readers
0-689-31890-0

❑ OUTRAGEOUSLY ALICE
Atheneum Books for Young Readers
0-689-80354-0
Aladdin Paperbacks 0-689-80596-9

❑ ALICE IN LACE
Atheneum Books for Young Readers
0-689-80358-3
Aladdin Paperbacks 0-689-80597-7

❑ ALICE THE BRAVE
Atheneum Books for Young Readers
0-689-80095-9
Aladdin Paperbacks 0-689-80598-5

❑ ACHINGLY ALICE
Atheneum Books for Young Readers
0-698-80533-9
Aladdin Paperbacks 0-689-80595-0
Simon Pulse 0-689-86396-9

❑ ALICE ON THE OUTSIDE
Atheneum Books for Young Readers
0-689-80359-1

❑ GROOMING OF ALICE
Atheneum Books for Young Readers
0-689-82633-8
Simon Pulse 0-689-84618-5

❑ ALICE ALONE
Atheneum Books for Young Readers
0-689-82634-6
Simon Pulse 0-689-85189-8

❑ SIMPLY ALICE
Atheneum Books for Young Readers
0-689-84751-3
Simon Pulse 0-689-85965-1

❑ STARTING WITH ALICE
Atheneum Books for Young Readers
0-689-84395-X

❑ PATIENTLY ALICE
Atheneum Books for Young Readers
0-689-82636-2

❑ ALICE IN BLUNDERLAND
Atheneum Books for Young Readers
0-689-84397-6